Praise for Charlene Teglia's **The Gripping Beast**!

4 Hearts! *"This tale of a rock star sent into the past by a magic armband is very engrossing. The author describes Viking times so well that you can almost picture yourself on the longboat. Lorelei and Erik are never boring, always challenging each other. Lorelei helps Erik find his sense of humor as well as love Her difficulties with slavery are at times sad, frustrating, or funny. ...I picked this one up and did not put it down until the last page. This is a very involving story."* ~ Maura Frankman, The Romance Studio

Blue Ribbon Rating: 4 *"THE GRIPPING BEAST is a great book full of action and adventure that readers will dive into and stay until the very end. Lorelei is a great heroine and stands up to Erik no matter what. Erik is a Viking with an alpha attitude that will knock your socks off... The love scenes are intense and very heated. Charlene Teglia has a knack for creating wonderful stories with interesting characters that will keep readers coming back for more."* ~ Angel Brewer, Romance Junkies

"I very much enjoyed The Gripping Beast! It's a well-written romantic tale that captivated me from the beginning. Erik and Lorelei are strong characters... I would happily be Erik's slave anywhere! Their passion, while being intense, is both carnal and sensual. I laughed, then I sighed and had tears in my eyes at the end. The Gripping Beast is a book I intend to read again and again!" ~ Nannette, Joyfully Reviewed

4.5 Stars *"Ms. Teglia has created the ideal time travel story that is filled with virile and lusty characters and touched with a love that sets the tone for a wonderfully romantic ride. By the end of this novel, I had no doubt these two were in love and felt*

their connection in every passage. Their sex scenes are extremely passionate, owing to the "fight and make up" sex that can set a delicious carnal scene on fire. Ms. Teglia has written such a smooth novel that I found myself at the end before I knew what happened. Those readers who enjoy Viking novels or time travel experiences will find The Gripping Beast a delightfully splendid read." - Francesca Hayne, Just Erotic Romance Reviews

THE GRIPPING BEAST is time travel fantasy at its best. This tale is a page turner and I recommend it to readers who love this genre. Charlene Teglia is quickly working her way onto my automatic buy list. She's truly a talented and promising author." - Vicki Turner, Romance Reviews Today

"A Five Pink Hats Off Salute to Charlene Teglia, for a knock your socks off story full of strong personalities that actually mesh. As Lorelei is swept back into time, she didn't expect to be swept off her feet also. She is a strong heroine - with a protected soft side. Erik, the handsome hero is a domineering type, determined to break down her wall. This is a book of perfection. For those that love Vikings, The Gripping Beast will have you riding a roller coaster of emotions." – BCJ, The Pink Posse

THE GRIPPING BEAST

BEAST

By Charlene Teglia

A Samhain Publishing, Ltd. publication

Samhain Publishing, Ltd.
PO Box 2206
Stow OH 44224

The Gripping Beast
Copyright © 2006 by Charlene Teglia
Cover by Scott Carpenter
Print ISBN: 1-59998-055-X
Digital ISBN: 1-59998-005-3
www.samhainpublishing.com

First electronic publication: February 2006

THE GRIPPING BEAST

BEAST

By Charlene Teglia

Dedication

This book is dedicated to my own real-life hero, Pat, who bugged me for years to finish it so he could read it, and to Crissy and Angie who bought it so I had to. Thank you!

Prologue

"Stop, start over. It's too slow. You're dragging by almost a full quarter-beat." The usually smoky, sultry voice rang with annoyance.

"I am not. You're rushing," snapped another feminine voice in response.

"Lorelei never rushes, everyone knows that," a dry alto interrupted in defense of the first voice. "She has a metronome in her head. If Lorelei says you're off, you're off. Pick it up and start from the top."

The snare snapped a down-beat and the bass and lead guitar swung in, perfectly coordinated this time. The slim, raven-haired lead vocalist nodded in approval and came in on cue.

It sent chills through their listening manager. Lorelei's music was riveting. She composed complex rhythmic structures that demanded perfectly timed execution. Combined with clean licks and soaring vocals that covered a full three-octave range, she'd sent the Sirens straight to the top of the charts from their very first release.

A release date she'd insisted on.

It was frustrating, but she dictated when to release a song or an album and when to tour. The other members protested from time to time, but in the end they always went along with her, because she was always right.

He'd never forgotten the one time he'd tried to insist on a concert Lorelei didn't want to do. "Bad idea," she'd said. And she wouldn't budge. In a freak storm, the stage they would have been on was struck by lightning, but Lorelei and the Sirens were unscathed— because they weren't there.

After that, he didn't argue with Lorelei, either.

As always, listening to the band perform was an experience, even for a seasoned pro. In addition to perfect timing and impeccable rhythm, Lorelei had an ability to project emotion through music that came through even in a recording.

Live, it was nothing less than electrifying. She made an audience feel everything she felt, from tears to laughter, and it was an industry joke that with the trademark sultry finish, hotels near any stadium the Sirens played did a brisk business after the concert.

Tonight would be the final performance of their celebrated Legends tour, with their opening act, Thor's Hammer.

Everything was in place. Everything was going perfectly. The show was sold out. He should have been a very happy manager.

Instead, he was distinctly nervous, because something was bothering Lorelei. And when Lorelei was on edge, something was about to go wrong.

Chapter One

"Lovely Lorelei, come and while away the time with me."

Lorelei Michaels stopped short at the invitation and let her eyes travel over six feet and four inches of buff, blond babe. Dane Larsen was two hundred and twenty pounds of scrumptious Scandinavian sex appeal in very attractive packaging. Muscles to drool over, a face to dream about, a throaty voice and that warm glint of humor in his eyes didn't hurt, either.

She looked at him and wondered what was wrong with her that she couldn't fall in love with a certified hunk like Dane.

"Come on," he teased. "I'll give you one of my famous back rubs. You're so edgy I could use you for an envelope opener."

She had to smile at his description. "Am I that bad?"

"Well, personally, I like a woman with sharp edges," Dane kidded. "It makes life interesting. But if you go on like that, you'll project it to the crowd and we'll have a riot instead of the usual Siren-induced love fest."

She shot him a killing look that he only laughed off. "See? You've misplaced your sense of humor. Come on, I'll cheer you up." The bass player flexed his strong fingers invitingly.

A back rub sounded wonderful, actually. She was tense. A mass of jangling nerves, to be more specific. And there was no obvious reason for it. The Legends tour was going so well. She knew without a hint of ego the album was going to go platinum.

It was her best work to date, and every stop on the tour they'd played to a sold-out crowd.

She was nearing the pinnacle of achievement in her career. She had success, recognition, money. She had youth, health and beauty. She had a gift and the joy of using it as it was meant to be used, to give others pleasure.

She should have been happy.

Instead, she was increasingly lost inside, edgy and restless. Looking for something and she wasn't even sure what.

No, if she was honest, she was looking for someone, and beginning to wonder if he existed. Why couldn't that someone be Dane? He was nice as well as gorgeous and they'd become good friends on the tour. Today wouldn't be the first time the bassist for their opening act, Thor's Hammer, had soothed her nerves and teased her back into good humor. In fact, Lorelei didn't know how she would have gotten through the grueling schedule without him.

"Dane, that's an offer I can't refuse." She smiled and fell into step with him. They slipped companionable arms around each other as they walked.

"So what was it today? Meghan off on the dragged triplets again?"

Lorelei groaned. "Oh, did you have to bring that up? Yes, I don't know why she falls off tempo on those, but I hate to take them out. They add so much to the texture of the song."

"Cry For Me", one of her favorites, had a particularly difficult opening that had the bass carry the melody in a series of minor dragged triplets. Meghan Davis, the Siren's bass player, seemed to have a mental block on that section and fluffed it repeatedly. Lorelei supposed she could always invert the bass and guitar parts and have Paige carry it, but she'd written it for bass for a reason and it irritated her to have to settle for anything less than her original composition.

And thinking about it wasn't doing anything to soothe her nerves or improve her mood.

Giving in to impulse, Lorelei jumped and landed in Dane's arms, knowing he'd catch her. "I don't want to talk about work. I want to be distracted. Distract me, Dane." .

He smiled back at her and swung her in a dizzy circle before returning her to her feet. "Gladly. And I have just the thing for you, too. You're going to love it."

"A surprise?"

"A fabulous surprise. It'll knock you out. Come on, I'll show you."

"What? What?" She danced beside him in excitement. "Give me a hint."

The tall blond slanted a gleeful look at her. "You want a hint? I'll give you a hint, but you'll never guess. Never, never, never."

"Ha! Try me."

"You asked for it. Here it is: the gripping beast." Smug satisfaction sounded in Dane's voice.

"Gripping beast? What's that? Is that a hint?" Lorelei demanded.

"That's all the hint you're getting."

"No fair! What kind of a hint is that? I demand a real hint."

"That's a real hint. You just don't know what it is and you won't guess, either," Dane gloated.

She fumed and shot him fiery looks. To no avail. Then she tried softening and coaxing. "Please, Dane. Please, please, please. Give me another hint."

He was unmoved by her wheedling. "No, you got one hint and that's all you get. Do you give up?"

"Never! I don't give up. It isn't in my vocabulary."

"Yeah, I know. But you aren't getting around me, so either take your best shot, or concede defeat." He smirked at her.

She considered him narrowly. "Gripping beast. That's what you said, right, the gripping beast?"

"Uh huh."

Lorelei ran through her mental repertoire of mythology, legends, folklore and music, but came up dry. Much as she hated to admit it, Dane had her stumped this time. But pride demanded she at least take a shot at it. "A new kind of glue."

He shouted with laughter, almost deafening her in the process. "Wrong!"

"A guitar stand."

"Way wrong."

She frowned. "What really old peanut butter becomes."

"Give it up, Lorelei, you don't know and you won't guess."

She gave him an exasperated look. "Okay, tell me."

He grinned at her. "I have to tell you a story first."

She brightened. "A myth?" She loved myths. She was an avid student of folklore and drew on cultural myths and legends frequently for musical themes. With her mixed heritage of Algonquin and Irish, she'd grown up hearing stories that never failed to delight her. She often wished she had the talent for storytelling, but since she didn't, she settled for reading everything she could get her hands on and listening to oral traditions every chance she got.

"Yeah, a family tale of weirdness sure to thrill you."

"Oh, a skeleton in the family closet? Tell away," Lorelei invited, intrigued.

"Not a skeleton, a lack of a skeleton, actually," Dane mused.

"You've got me hanging. I'm all ears."

"Lovely ears they are, too. Well, come into my dressing room." He opened the door and indicated she should precede him.

Lorelei threw herself full-length onto the convenient couch, face down, her head pillowed on her folded arms in preparation for a phenomenal back rub.

She wasn't disappointed. In fact, as Dane flexed his fingers and kneaded her shoulders, she shot him a questioning look. "You? Is that the answer to the riddle?"

He smiled back. "No, it's not me, but I'm forever flattered that you thought of me in terms of a beast." He continued to work along the line towards her neck. "With all this tension, you should have a raging headache. I thought you were still working out to relax."

"Um, doing tai chi. I am, and it helps. You should try me when I miss a day." The wry note in her voice served as an admission of her awareness that she was less than pleasant to be around these days.

"Just think, you can give Meghan a toss over your shoulder if she messes up again. That should relax you."

Lorelei smiled unwillingly. "That's a terrible thing to say. Although I can't deny that it's crossed my mind on one or two occasions. But really, a band is a team and she's good. It's not her fault I'm so on edge."

"And why are you on edge?"

Eyes closed, Lorelei missed the look that fleetingly crossed her friend's face. A look of longing and resignation quickly masked behind a smiling facade.

"I don't really know," she answered slowly. "Well, I do, but it sounds so ridiculous. Everything is going right. But the more it does, the more I get the feeling that it's all wrong somehow."

He paused, serious for a moment. "Do you have one of your feelings about tonight?"

She opened troubled eyes to meet his. "No. Not exactly. It's more about me, and it keeps getting worse." She hesitated briefly. "All right, I'll tell you but you'd better promise not to sell the story to the media. Inquiring minds do *not* need to know."

Dane's face took on an expression of wounded innocence and she made a face at him. "Cut it out. Okay, Dane, here it is. Lorelei Michaels, seductive temptress and siren singer of love and passion, is a fake."

He pretended to consider that and prodded her side with one finger. "I don't know, you feel pretty real to me."

She grinned as much at his tickling as his teasing. "Fool. No, really, all these songs about love and desire and heartbreak are probably my repressed libidinous urges finding an outlet."

He gave her a wicked look. "Oh, is this a personal problem I can help you with? As a devoted friend?"

Lorelei laughed. "You're so generous. But really, what's wrong with me that I can't respond to anybody? I remember all those rumors about Jim Morrison, how his sexy act was all a show and in real life he was impotent. At least in his case it could be explained by drugs. What's my excuse?"

As she put it into words, she felt the hurt and self-doubt all over again. At first she'd told herself she just hadn't met the right person. She wasn't ready. The chemistry wasn't right. The timing wasn't right. But time went on, and nothing changed.

Don't say it, she warned herself, don't even think the "f" word...frigid. She couldn't really believe it. She had passion. It came through so clearly in her work and in her overall approach to life. So why didn't she feel it for a man?

Dane stopped and pushed her over to make room on the couch before he joined her. "Lorelei, what makes you think anything's wrong with you? So you aren't a megaslut. That's bad?" He went on jokingly, "Okay, maybe to the male fans, it's bad. There are a lot of disappointed men in your life. But why is it wrong to want to wait for something special?"

Lorelei curled against his side. "Because it's probably a cop-out. Emotional cowardice. I'm holding out for perfection so I never have to take a risk," she muttered in self-condemnation.

Dane laughed dryly. "I think you're pretty rough on yourself. I've never known a musician who pushed harder and took more risks. You don't do anything by traditional methods. If you think it might work, you go for it, and you don't hold back. It's what's made you so successful. And I think some day, some lucky man is going to make you want to risk everything and give your whole heart and soul." He gave her an affectionate cuff on the shoulder. "You'll do it, too. You never do anything halfway."

The warmth and caring concern mingled with admiration in his voice did as much as the words to comfort her. An answering warmth welled up and she hugged him. "Thanks. You're some friend, you know that?"

She didn't see the sadness in his eyes as he looked down at her bent head.

He would have given almost anything to be the one Lorelei was looking for, but he knew very well it would never be. She would never see him as anything but a friend. Still, her friendship was worth a lot and he was willing to settle for being her buddy. If all she wanted was a friend, he'd be that friend. Out loud he said only, "Yeah, I know that."

He went on, "As your friend, I promised you a stunning distraction. Prepare to be amazed."

"Oh, I'm ready. Amaze me."

"Well, you know I'm descended from Vikings."

"Yes, I read your bio," Lorelei teased. "Nice press releases you get. Nice coverage, too. Or should I say, lack of coverage? Especially that shot of you with—"

"All right," he broke in with a hunted look. "Enough about me. This is about my family."

"Coward." Lorelei delivered the accusation in a challenging tone. It was a well-known fact to any mythology buff that Thor's hammer was a masculine fertility symbol, and that particular picture of Dane had been truly spectacular symbolism.

Dane let her challenge pass without comment and went on with his story. "Well, this is about an old Viking wedding ceremony. The bride wore one of the groom's armbands and they drank from the same cup. You've heard of this?"

Lorelei nodded, enjoying her distraction immensely.

"Then here's the story. A Viking ancestor captured a Valkyrie. She was brave and beautiful, and she admired the Viking's strength. She fell in love with the mortal, and he married her. But when they drank from the same cup and he gave her the armband, they both vanished. The armband fell to the ground, supposedly because she wasn't mortal and couldn't hold on to it. But she took her warrior with her, back to Valhalla."

Dane paused and Lorelei tugged at his arms in impatience. "That can't be all. Don't stop. What happened?"

He frowned down at her. "Patience is a virtue."

Lorelei frowned back. "Oh, like I need lectures on virtue from the guy who showed the world his——"

"Okay," Dane interrupted again. "Here's the rest of the story. I have the armband."

Lorelei sat up. "No. You're kidding me. You mean you really do have it? Show me, please?"

"Sure thing. In fact, I'll do one better. I'll let you wear it," he offered.

"Really? Oh, Dane, that's incredible." She leaned forward and kissed his cheek in excitement. "Where is it?"

"Right here." The blond man reached into his deep vest pocket and drew out a barbaric and beautiful example of Viking jewelry.

"Oh," Lorelei said in awe. She reached out to touch it, finding it heavy. "It's solid, isn't it?"

"Yes, solid silver-plated with gold in the design. That's your clue, babe." Dane took her hand and traced her fingers over the intricate metalwork that depicted strange animals entwined.

"My clue. The gripping beast?"

"Uh huh. It doesn't have a name on record, but art historians call it that. It's part cat, part reptile and part weasel, always shown entwined in a figure like this, gripping each other with their paws." Dane grinned at her as she absorbed that bit of information, enjoying her enthusiasm.

She slowly traced the design again. "Hm, you know it reminds me of the Egyptian idea about time and infinity. A snake with its tail in its mouth."

"Well, what better symbol for a legendary love story?" Dane teased. He placed it in her hand and closed her fingers over the wide band. "Tonight, it's yours. Wear it and may it inspire you to sing of love like never before," he intoned in a mock blessing.

Lorelei laughed up at him. "And may my opening act fire up the crowd. Especially when they see your, uh, hammer."

"Lorelei, your cruelty will someday come back to haunt you. I have the story inquiring minds want to know," Dane reminded her in a voice filled with dark threat.

"Yeah, but you don't have the pictures," she snickered.

He frowned and shook a fist at her.

"Hey, that reminds me, how did you get this little memento?" Lorelei asked, jolted back to the subject. "This isn't one of those little jokes of yours, is it? You didn't happen to borrow this from a museum collection?"

Dane leaned back and folded his arms. "I've just been insulted by a fraudulent siren."

"Really. Tell me I'm not going to go out there in this and get arrested."

"You won't get arrested. It's mine. It's been handed down in the family since something like the beginning of time. It's certainly old enough. Anyway, now it's been handed down to me and there's nobody I'd rather see wear it than you." He pushed back one raven wing of hair and kissed her forehead. "It suits you, you were made for that kind of stuff. And you love it. So go on, play Valkyrie and have fun."

Lorelei tipped her face back to consider that. "Isn't that mixing my legends? I can't be a Siren and a Valkyrie at the same time. I'd be kicked out of the myths network. I'm already in trouble for having three other band members when the traditional Siren count is three, total. Two if you go by Homer. Four is really pushing it." She frowned and pretended grave concern.

Dane grinned. "I think you're officially distracted. You're definitely back to your usual happy self. Mix all the myths you want, you'll always be a legend in my book." He tousled her hair and stood. "Come on, babe, we need to get ready. It's almost show time."

Lorelei stood and stretched in a graceful, sinuous movement, her dark hair sweeping around her waist. She held up the armband and smiled slowly at Dane. "This is what I call heavy metal."

The piece was really heavy, and large enough to give her some idea of the original owner's build. He'd evidently had some bulging biceps to wear the band without it sliding off.

No wonder the Valkyrie had dropped it, she thought with quick humor. It would slide right off of her, too. Maybe the Vikings were the first body builders, wielding their heavy swords in lieu of free weights.

"Funny, Lorelei, very funny," Dane returned, looking pained at her poor pun.

"You don't like heavy metal?"

"You sing it and I'll like it," he vowed mock-seriously. "Listen, I have to go now, being the lowly opener. Are you all right?"

She nodded. "I'm all right. Thanks, Dane. Me and my heavy metal band will wow the crowd. You go wow 'em with your hammer."

The big blond threw back his head and laughed. "Just for you, I'll do that," he promised, a glint of devilment in his eyes promising trouble ahead.

Alarmed, Lorelei called after him, "Hey, don't do anything like indecent exposure! If you get arrested, we'll have to do an extra set."

He waved back at her in acknowledgment, but she noticed he didn't make any promises. An unwilling smile tugged at her mouth. He played on his heritage, putting on a wild, barbarian show, but he was a good guy underneath. She literally couldn't count the times she'd seen him go out of his way to help other people in the business, and he'd gone way beyond the bounds of friendship for her repeatedly.

She should write him a song, Lorelei reflected. A "Thank You for Being a Friend" kind of thing, a powerhouse hit in honor of his powerful presence. With subtle references to his hammer. She giggled at the idea. He'd blush. Although a man who posed for a picture like that should be beyond embarrassment.

It was odd that Dane was the personality of Thor's Hammer, instead of the lead vocalist, the usual front person. He just didn't have the kind of personality that blended into the background. The singer, Bjorn, was much more intense, and the two had an interesting mix of control and wildness between them that made the band unique.

It always fascinated her, the endless combinations of complexities that emerged from meshing different people with different personalities and backgrounds in music. Each added their own individual flavor, but the whole was always more than the sum of the parts. Music had a way of crossing boundaries and creating unity and harmony.

As long as the musicians checked their egos at the stage door, Lorelei acknowledged wryly. Unfortunately, too many failed to do that, and they never lasted as a result. Personality conflicts destroyed too many partnerships that could have been star quality. Sadly, the egomaniacs never reached anything close to their potential in a solo career.

Lorelei had seen it too often to allow herself to fall into the same trap. Her songwriting talent shaped the band in many ways, and she led in business decisions as well, but she never forgot how important the rest of the team was.

Paige Reynolds, lead guitarist and Southern belle, added a sweetness to their music. Meghan, with her hard-as-nails persona, had intensity and gave the bass a wickedly sharp, nasty edge. Maybe that was why the melancholy dragged triplets gave her a problem, Lorelei mused absently. They called for a soft, emotional approach. Then their new drummer, Lisa Atkins, who'd joined them after the original percussionist wanted out, had ferocious tenacity and never lost the thread of the rhythmic patterns that interwove the music and made it all hang together.

Lorelei might write and arrange them, but she couldn't play intricate compositions solo. Together, the four women made a top band with years of solid performances ahead. Solo, they'd be back to struggling and they were all smart enough to know it.

They'd all struggled enough in the garages and bars of Seattle's music scene, until Lorelei put them together and proposed the Sirens, using the mythical concept as an appealing romantic image. They'd seen the advantages immediately and worked hard to get a demo and debut album. The rest was history.

Including Sara, the first drummer. A pang of loss accompanied the thought. Sara, with her constant laughter and generous heart had taken one look at fame and said no. The lifestyle didn't suit her. She didn't have the tough shell to endure the limelight or the separations from her husband. The whole band had cried when she decided to quit, but they couldn't hold her to an agreement that made her miserable.

Thinking of Sara, Lorelei wondered what she was doing now, and if she'd be watching the recorded concert on MTV tonight.

"I miss you, Sara," she murmured out loud. "I'll sing to you tonight."

Then she traced the mythical animal design again and smiled.

She'd sing to Dane, her friend, distracter, and fan.

She'd sing to the nameless yearning and lose her frustration and gnawing emptiness in music. Her restless impatience stirred again at the thought, insisting that it was time. It was past time.

And past time for her to get ready. If she didn't get moving, she'd be demoted back to singing in the shower.

Lorelei slipped to her room and grabbed the change of clothing hanging ready, a soft and romantic sea foam green dress, tightly fitted at the top in a body-hugging knit with a gauzy net skirt. The sea-born, ethereal look set off her long raven hair and lit up her eyes, making her look like the Lorelei of legend. The siren who lured men to their doom.

She dressed and touched up her make-up, already done earlier for the stage lighting. It seemed dark and overdone in the light of her dressing room, but it would pale under the intense lights to look street normal.

Green sequined shoes slipped over silky stockings, and she was in Siren uniform. She started breathing deeply, expanding and contracting her diaphragm and worked her jaw in a series of warm-up exercises before lightly trilling a set of three- and five-note scales, then octave intervals to warm up her voice.

Another example of her obsession for details. She wasn't about to become an ex-rocker with a voice ruined from lack of care.

Warmed up and dressed, Lorelei paused to take a look in the full-length mirror. She was in costume and in character, and she felt ready.

She also felt terribly alone.

In fierce defiance of the feeling, she picked up Dane's armband and slipped her hand through it. Maybe the symbol of power and ferocity from another time might lend her the strength to carry her through the night.

She couldn't help thinking of the armband's history as she slid it on. The Viking and Valkyrie who'd loved each other, vanished together, were still together in some other place, maybe. Legendary love. Forever love. And suddenly all her stormy emotions, her restless discontent, the sense of something missing boiled up inside her and found expression in a single concentrated wish. *I want that.*

Funny, the band seemed cold to the touch now that she was wearing it. Much colder than she'd remembered when she first picked it up. The cold shock of the metal sent a chill down her arm and through her body. So cold, it even seemed to block out the distant vibrations of bass and percussion.

Lorelei glanced down at the strange, writhing animal design she wore and thought she saw the reptilian links sliding and twisting. It seemed to recede, too, moving much too far away. Her vision narrowed until she could see nothing else. Then even that image melted away in a halo of glaring light. A whirling, roaring cone of light gripped her and pulled her relentlessly down.

Chapter Two

Erik scowled at his younger brother and reminded himself sternly that he was a good and dutiful son.

He had a duty to uphold the family honor. He could not give free rein to his temper and take the flat side of his sword to the troublesome, thoughtless, thoroughly exasperating family member entrusted to his care.

Still, it was only with the greatest effort that he kept his voice calm as he once again attempted to acquaint Harold with the notion that a true Viking did not take with his sword everything that caught his eye. A Viking was always ready, true. But a wise leader sought a more stable solution than quick gain by force.

Erik knew well that such quick gains inevitably met equally rapid losses. But perhaps that was the difference in years between them. For all his bluster and size, Harold was still little more than a boy, while Erik was well into manhood and further tempered by the burdens of responsibility as well as experience.

Although from the perspective of his great age of five and twenty, Erik did not recall being so carefree nor quite so hotheaded as Harold at any age. It was indeed difficult to believe a bare four years separated the two of them.

"You would do well to look for an advantage in trade, not battle," Erik lectured as he kept a firm grip on Harold's broad shoulder and drew him along. Harold would do even better to learn to think before acting, he continued silently.

Harold responded with the crooked smile that never failed to charm a woman and was indirectly responsible for the fact that Erik was stuck with him for the summer.

"Brother, where is the fun in that? Four long weeks I've spent, watching you haggle in the marketplace. It lacks excitement. If that is all you come to Hedeby for, you may continue alone. I for one must have some sport before I find myself at sea with you once more."

His intent was clear in the longing gaze he fixed on a curvaceous wench.

Erik sighed inwardly. A woman was the reason for Harold's banishment from home for the summer. Apparently, he had failed to learn a lesson from the beating Gudred's brother had given him for stealing a kiss.

The reminder that Harold was not alone in his needs irked him further. But duty must come first, Erik reminded himself. While he had nearly completed his trading, he thought he might still find some small and profitable items to add to the goods already loaded onto his longboat in exchange for its former cargo of rich Northern furs, amber and falcons.

"There will be time for that when the ice keeps us home." Erik delivered the firm reminder with a stern look.

Then he cursed his choice of words inwardly. If Harold did not learn to behave himself at home, his penchant for indiscriminate wenching and brawling would soon have him outlawed and banished permanently. Their father, Thorolf, might be jarl, but he could ill afford failure to enforce the laws on his own family.

The northern summers didn't last long, and it was only once a year that they could venture out on the long trading voyages so vital to the prosperity of the Norse settlements. Cloth they couldn't weave themselves like the fine brocades from the Byzantine, patterned silks from China and the blue wools dyed with woad from Frisia were much in demand, as were the spices, metals and leather goods to be found in the large trade centers.

"You are well acquainted with ice," Harold muttered under his breath in reply.

But he followed Erik's wide strides along the wooden planking that covered the muddy streets.

Then he brightened, seeing the direction Erik was taking, a direct route to a slaver displaying his wares. "Ah, I take it back," he teased. "I see we think alike after all."

Erik paused to shoot a mistrustful glance at Harold. "You have an interest in trade now?"

"Of a certainty," his brother vowed.

Erik shook his head. He did not believe for the time it took to take one step that Harold shared his interest in the Egyptian glass works in the temporary tent set up between the town's permanent traders and the outer ramparts. The flattened glass oblongs were used to press pleats into linen skirts. The opportunity to supply such a fashionable novelty struck him as a good choice to round out his return cargo, likely to prove highly lucrative.

"Oh, by Thor, what a fine idea," Harold continued. He gave Erik an affectionate clout which that recipient longed to return in force. "I like the look of that one." Harold waved a cheerful hand towards a group of girls that stood between the two men and their goal.

Erik sighed inwardly again. He might have known. The day Harold grew interested in serious matters, Loki would be running loose and Ragnarok would begin. He doubted that Harold had even noticed the Egyptian's tent the previous day.

"So does the crowd," Harold went on. "He is offering her up first. What an odd dress she has on," he added in surprise. "Perhaps she comes from the far east."

Distracted from his purpose, Erik stared first at his brother, then at the object of his attention.

The foreign woman was indeed dressed oddly. And very beautifully. The flowing green gauze hid little and the upper part of the dress, if it was a dress, revealed even more. Erik felt his heart slam against the wall of his chest and stop.

Beautiful. She was a vision of loveliness. Erik had never seen a woman with the look she had, not in any part of the world he had visited. Sleek black hair fell in a glossy swath to her narrow waist and light green eyes sparkled like emeralds above exotic high cheekbones.

He didn't realize he had come to a complete halt and was gaping at the dark woman like a man ensorcelled. He knew only that she was beauty come warmly to life, and at that moment he wanted nothing more than to simply look at her for the rest of his days. That was his only thought, until he realized that every other man, save a blind beggar, was looking at her, also. And that the slaver, probably thinking to get a higher price for her, had ordered her to strip.

He wasn't quite certain what happened next, and perhaps it all happened simultaneously. The man put his hands on her. She started to shriek and fight like a berserker. And Erik drew his sword.

He didn't notice when his brother and the crew, trailing behind them, followed suit. He didn't know they took up his roar of rage and charged into the fight at his lead.

He only knew he would kill every man standing who saw what he wanted for himself alone.

The hapless slave trader might never know what provoked the Vikings to charge down on him, but he demonstrated an instinct for self-protection as he thrust the woman between his own body and the crazed Norse giant ready to cleave him with a sword.

Through a red haze of fury, Erik caught the woman around her waist and yanked her against his side as he thrust the point of his sword against the coward's throat. Then a thread of sanity returned and stayed his arm.

He could not start a bloodbath in the trade port.

He could not set such a terrible example for Harold. As it was, he cursed inwardly at the sight of his delighted sibling exchanging blows with a burly Moor. And his men. They lived in adjoining farmsteads. They looked to his father for leadership, and expected him to prove himself a worthy leader.

He would not lead them into lawlessness. The days of going Viking were in the past. With the establishment of the Danelaw and the treaty with Alfred of Wessex, as well as the settlement in Normandy by conquering raiders, peaceful trade replaced plundering as a means for gaining wealth.

Decided, Erik flipped a silver coin in the air and slashed sideways with his sword.

The halved coin fell at the slaver's feet. He felt at his throat as if checking to be certain it was intact before he reached down for the coin.

"Half," Erik grated out in rough Arabic.

"All," the man returned slyly, glancing around. "I'll need to replace the girl. Do you think I can make an honest living in this way?"

It was the wrong tactic. A flash of the ornate sword hacked the coin again and left one quarter lying in the dirt. The rest he handed to Harold. "The bargain is done," he stated, holding the cowardly little man's eyes.

Defeated, the man nodded.

Erik scanned the crowd gathered around the fighters with equal directness. There were no challenges. They'd witnessed the bargain struck.

Satisfied, he turned and strode to the tent displaying the flat glass oblongs and pointed at them. "I want some of these," he informed Harold, speaking Norse once more. "Take care of it and deliver them to the ship."

Then he left the Egyptian merchant facing the band of Vikings and made for his longboat with the woman under his arm like an unwieldy package.

Shaking with reaction, Lorelei pounded one fist on the big man's chest. "Stop. Wait," she wheezed out. "Did the director yell 'cut'?"

The man halted and looked down at her with a face so expressionless she wondered if he'd understood a word she said.

With a face that handsome, she guessed he could get away with failing to understand quite a bit. But something about the lines of character in his face and the deep blue of his eyes hinted at intelligence.

"This has to be a set," Lorelei babbled on. "I didn't see any barricades to mark it off and nobody asked me to sign a release form, but what other explanation is there? I mean, somebody's doing a remake of The Vikings, right? Kevin Costner is around here somewhere with a sword."

She stopped, closed her eyes and took a deep breath. "I'm not supposed to be here. I have a concert to do. I don't belong here. There's been some kind of mistake."

Maybe if she just closed her eyes, it would go away and she'd be back in her dressing room. Yes, that was definitely it. She'd just keep them closed another minute.

She reopened her eyes and met his again. Lorelei groped along his broad chest with both hands, then pinched him. He scowled at her in reaction.

"Sorry. I just wanted to see if you're real." She looked wildly around at the unfamiliar sea of faces and wondered if any of this was for real.

It couldn't be.

It couldn't be, so it wasn't, Lorelei decided.

She was hallucinating the whole thing. Even so, she ought to thank the man who'd come to her rescue. He'd arrived just in time to stop that slimy creep with the rotten teeth who'd tried to rip off her dress.

She hadn't understood anything the worm had said, but some things transcended language barriers. She didn't need a translator to know what he'd been after.

Lorelei shuddered again. "That was really horrible," she mumbled to the man. "Thank you for helping me. Even if you aren't real, it was still nice of you."

She patted his muscled chest gratefully. "Good hallucination."

Her head was reeling and everything seemed to be spinning slowly around them. She had the mother of all headaches. Lorelei frowned, squinted in an effort to bring the world into focus, then closed her eyes again. Something was really wrong. With her. That was it, she realized muzzily. If she was hallucinating men with swords, she must have been drugged somehow. Although if it made her hallucinate a gorgeous man like the one holding her, it wasn't all bad.

"Drugged," she informed the man holding her up in a distant voice. "Somebody must've slipped me something. S'the only explanation. Think I'm going to faint." Then she suited actions to words.

Erik frowned at the unconscious woman in his arms. What sort of drug had the trader given her? Perhaps he'd given her something to keep her quiet during the sale and miscalculated the dosage. He could only hope she hadn't been overdosed and that she would wake soon.

If she failed to wake, Erik vowed he would return to carve the little man into pieces after all.

He lifted her more fully into the cradle of his arms and continued on his way as he replaced the disquieting thought with immovable determination. He would not lose her. Not when he had just found her. She would wake, and she would be well, and she would cease to babble like a madwoman.

Where had she come from, that she spoke Norse so oddly? He could not think of any region that spoke with such an accent. She had somewhat the look of the Celts. Perhaps she had come from Ireland and learned the language from Vikings settled there.

Erik pushed the mystery from his mind for the present. It mattered little where she came from. She belonged to him now. He cared not how she came to be in Hedeby, or why the trader had needed to drug her. He smiled faintly, remembering how she had fought in spite of it.

Well, perhaps there was no mystery there. She could not have been a slave long. Slaves had no rights, not even the right to defend themselves. She had courage. Still, she would learn to behave as she should, he decided. She would not fight him.

A pleasing image grew and filled his thoughts, an image of the woman smiling and undressing at his command in sweet submission for him alone.

The image drew a twisting knot of need in his vitals. He had gained more than he had ever expected this day. A private playmate, a respite from endless duty, a source of brightness in his days to look forward to. As his slave, her sole duty would be to please him and to fulfill his every desire. Looking down at the woman in his arms gave rise to a number of desires for her to fulfill when she recovered from her swoon. A pleasurable anticipatory glow filled him and quickened his pace.

Erik was suddenly eager to be on his way home.

The dizziness and the headache were fading, but the glaring light wasn't. Lorelei frowned and turned her face to shade it from the brightness against the warm, smooth surface pillowing her head. Better. She sighed happily, and decided not to open her eyes just yet.

She thought she still felt traces of the odd dream she'd been having. She could smell a tang of salt in the air, as if she were back in that odd seaside village with those odd people.

Movie people, she remembered. She'd been on a movie set. Must have been something Morris, her manager, had set up for her. A new music video concept, probably.

Something aimed at the global market, she guessed from the foreign languages she'd heard and the outlandish costumes. Somebody had really gone overboard, there, Lorelei thought in disapproval. Some members of the cast hadn't even bathed. In her book, that was trying a little too hard for authenticity. Method actors, probably.

She rubbed her cheek luxuriously against the warm, protective shelter from the sun's glare again and delighted in the sensation. "Mm," she sighed and snuggled closer. When had she ever woken up feeling so good, so right?

Maybe it was safe to wake up now.

Lorelei opened her eyes. And screamed.

Jackknifing off of the lap she'd been on, she leaped to her feet, her eyes still fixed on the armband that was identical to the one Dane had given her. The one she was no longer wearing.

Only it wasn't worn and tarnished with age.

It was new.

The heavily muscled male arm, now wearing the decorative band, along with the rest of the large body Lorelei remembered from their sword-waving encounter, moved towards her and clamped a firm hand over her mouth.

"Cease."

Cooperating wasn't exactly what she felt like doing, but Lorelei cut off the scream anyway since risking scar tissue on her vocal cords didn't seem like a good idea, either.

What did the man expect, she wondered in irritation, calm? Did he think she saw sword fights every day? And what was the trick with the armband?

Cool blue eyes bore into hers and Lorelei met them with a faint nod to indicate that she understood.

Although she didn't.

She didn't understand a thing, and she'd never felt more like screaming in her life.

It obviously wasn't a movie set that she'd been on.

Then she saw the outline of sea and sky and recognized the rocking motion of the floor underneath her feet. Panic struck again as she leaped to one conclusion, then another.

She was on a ship. And she'd been kidnapped. By a bunch of guys in costume, which really made no sense.

A familiar masculine laugh caught her attention. "You see, brother? Your scowling face has her fleeing. I knew she was a woman of wit."

Lorelei swung her head in the direction the voice had come from and felt relief flood her. "*Dane.*" Without hesitation, she tore loose from the unnerving sword-wielder and hurled herself towards the one familiar person near her. "Dane, am I ever happy to see you. But how did you get here? Am I still dreaming? Is this a Wizard of Oz kind of dream with everybody I know in it?"

He laughed uproariously and hugged her. "She likes me, I think," he informed the other man. "Perhaps she thinks you do not look enough like a Dane to suit her tastes."

Lorelei pulled back and glared at Dane. "Very funny. Cut it out, will you? I knew you were up to something with that armband." She pointed to the object in question, or rather, the pair of them, now worn by the big man who did indeed have bulging biceps—as she'd suspected, from the size of the bands.

He was even bigger than Dane. And that he lacked Dane's sense of humor was alarmingly obvious. Without the familiar teasing expression to soften his harsh features or the warmth of laughter in his hard gaze, he looked like an older, colder nightmare version of her friend.

Lorelei shivered, suddenly aware of her slight size in comparison.

The man could snap her in half like a twig. And he looked like he wanted to.

Great going, she groaned silently. You had to get snatched by Attila the Hunk. Probably some crazy survivalist fanatic, judging by the sword he wore and his readiness to use it.

"What do you want with me?" Lorelei demanded. "Shouldn't you be out building bomb shelters or something?" Too late, she realized she probably shouldn't be antagonizing the man who was obviously the leader and whose good will her life just might depend on.

They should have kidnapped Paige. She knew how to get along with anyone under any circumstances. Not that she'd wish anyone in her shoes just then.

Well, she wasn't Southern and she wasn't sweet, but maybe she could try to make some sense of all of this. Starting with why Dane was cooperating with kidnappers.

Some semblance of reason reasserted itself then. Dane wouldn't be cooperating with kidnappers. There was a reasonable explanation for the whole thing, and she should calm down and try to find out what it was. Lorelei took a deep breath, and turned back to Dane.

"What gives?" she demanded, poking his chest for emphasis and pushing her face close to his, the better to glare at him.

The sword-waving maniac growled and yanked her away from Dane. "You will give him nothing. Understand?" the man snarled.

Lorelei blinked. Then nodded. Then shook her head. "No, I'm afraid I don't understand." She tilted her face towards Dane again and bit out, "This little joke of yours has gone far enough. Tell Conan here to let go of me, and then start explaining."

Conan tightened his grip and said very softly, "My name is not Conan. I am Erik, but you will call me Master."

Lorelei couldn't help it. She laughed.

"Oh, dear," she managed to gasp out. "Now I know I'm not the one who's dreaming. Master!" She laughed harder, until her knees turned weak and she sagged against the man. Then she continued to giggle helplessly. "Master. You're killing me. That's the funniest thing I've heard in a long time." She giggled some more, then managed to get a grip and straighten up to address the two, since the rest of the men seemed content to watch and listen.

"Okay, let's get serious, guys. Somebody tell me what's going on. And you can start with this." She pointed at the telltale armband on Master Conan's arm and waited.

The two men looked at each other. Then the one who wanted to be called Master snarled, "What have you done, little brother?"

Dane looked deeply offended. "Not a thing. I have not touched it."

Lorelei snorted derisively. "You did so. You gave it to me. You told me to wear it. Are you having memory blackouts or something?"

Dane scowled at her, then at Conan. "I swear to you, brother, I have done nothing. I do not know this woman."

"Oh, you do, too, and I knew you were up to something." Lorelei frowned at him, then sat abruptly as the boat hit a swell. "I shouldn't have taken it. I knew you were setting me up," she accused, shooting Dane a reproachful look. "Now look what you've done," she added as water washed over the sides and drenched her.

Dane glared at her in disbelief. "You blame me for the actions of the ocean?"

She glared back. "I blame you for putting me here. This is all your fault. And to think I was going to write a song for you."

That got a reaction she didn't expect. The men all stared at her, and at Dane, looking shocked. Dane looked the most surprised.

"A song?" He croaked the words out, and she almost laughed again at the expression on his face. As if a song in his honor meant something very important.

"Yeah, but you can forget it now, you and Thor's Hammer," she snarled. She wrung water from her dress and brushed vainly at the fabric, then tried to smooth out her hair. She gave up in frustration. "Where's a mirror?" she pleaded, turning her face towards Conan. "I'm supposed to be onstage and I can't perform like this. Look at me. I'm a wreck."

He stared back at her, and she added on a moan, "Don't tell me you kidnapped me before the concert and you're making me miss it."

He didn't answer, and she sagged against the side of the boat, discouraged.

"This isn't fair, you know. In the Wizard of Oz, Dorothy had everyone she knew. I get stuck with Dane, but where's the rest of my band? And where's my manager, Morris? He's supposed to be here. What if I have a problem?" she demanded, waving her arms at Master Conan. "And I do have a problem. Am I supposed to do everything myself? That's what I pay him for. Why isn't he here to take care of this?"

Conan frowned at her fiercely. "Do I hear you aright? You demand your personal thralls?"

Lorelei blinked. "My what?"

He strode to stand over her, fists on his hips. "You will understand your position here," he informed her. "You do not have thralls. You are less than a thrall. You are my property."

Lorelei gazed back, then turned bewildered eyes to Dane. "Is this a board meeting? Is that what this is about?"

She'd incorporated the Sirens to simplify handling the business details, but still, it was a private venture. All the Sirens were co-owners. No, that didn't make any sense, either. The man who called her his property wasn't a board member and they hadn't sold any significant permanent rights to any outside concerns. She couldn't see how he could claim any ownership.

Unless he was as nutty as a fruitcake.

"Dane," she said calmly, "how could it possibly have escaped your notice that this man is a raving lunatic?"

Dane laughed.

The lunatic took offense at her statement. Not surprisingly.

"You will not slander me."

"It isn't slander if it's the truth," Lorelei retorted. "You've got bats in your belfry. You're a few bricks shy of a load. You're not playing with a full deck. Am I making myself clear? You're a runaway from a rubber room. A couch case. Delusional and who knows what else. A sword-wielding psycho." She ended her descriptive monologue with a disgusted wave at the offending sword.

The psycho scowled fiercely. "You will apologize for your slander, or you will be punished."

Lorelei hooted at that threat. "Punished? I'm already being punished. Besides, you really are nuts if you're saying what I think you're saying."

"What do you think I am saying?"

She held a hand towards him and he took it, pulling her to her feet. "Thanks." She brushed at her skirt, then gestured at his size. "Now, look at your fist."

Uncomprehending, he did.

"Then look at me," she continued.

He did that also.

"Now put the two together," she suggested. "You hit me with that once, and it'll be the last time."

He looked even more ferocious. "Do you threaten to run away? The punishment for escape is—"

"Don't tell me," she cut in. "Death by torture, right? You'll force me to listen to John Denver records until I beg for mercy. No, my large muscle-bound friend, I do not threaten to run away. I am simply pointing out the little fact that one love-tap from you is likely to put me to sleep for the last time." She patted him kindly. "Didn't think that one through, did you? If you really want to keep me, killing me is a bad plan."

Killing her was sounding better all the time. But she had the right of it. He dared not strike her, much as she deserved it for her insolence. Not that he would do such a thing. Had he not drawn his sword to protect her at the first sight of her? He had not gone to the trouble of taking her for his own to abuse her. Although to be fair, he acknowledged silently, she could not know what manner of man he was. Still, it pricked his pride and Erik vowed to silence her taunting tongue at the earliest opportunity.

She met his eyes calmly and added, "I want you to understand that I'm not going to cooperate with whatever plan you've cooked up."

Erik frowned. Nothing was cooking. Did she mock him again?

She went on, "You stole me. If you think I'm going to sing for you, you can think again." She drew herself up to her full height, which wasn't much in comparison, and gestured towards the longboat's covered storage hold. "I'll be in the cabin waiting while you boys decide what you're going to do."

Then she calmly walked away as if she had every right to do as she pleased, dismissing him completely.

Chapter Three

He was infuriating, Lorelei fumed.

She was so annoyed that it was a full ten minutes at least before her surroundings made any impact on her and she started to examine the contents of the odd room on the even odder boat.

Which was when it dawned on her that she'd never seen one like it. Or seen any boat with a red sail, come to think of it. And...had she really seen round shields along the sides? And were those men actually manning *oars*?

The clothes, those were really strange, too.

And Conan's sword. They all had swords, but his was a museum piece, even she could see that. The ornate figures and the intricate metalwork declared the sword's value even without the jeweled hilt. Where had he gotten a sword like that? Were the others similar?

She frowned, and realized something else was nagging at her. Something that wasn't quite right.

She hesitated, then stepped back out on the deck to take a good look at everything.

The nearest rower didn't protest when she peered closely at his clothing, then his sword. It was also fine workmanship, with decorative patterns etched in the blade. Lorelei looked him over carefully, then asked, "What's your name?"

The man smiled at her. "Bjarni."

"Barney," she echoed faintly. "Nice to meet you."

Conan came over, probably to continue their conversation, but she waved him away. "Not now, I have to see Dane."

Dane, fortunately, was right there, smiling his devilish smile. "You wish to see me?"

She nodded, looking back at him. There was something...

When she saw it, the shock made her stagger against Conan. She clutched at his arm for support automatically. "No," she muttered. "That isn't possible. It isn't."

For a long, frozen moment, she simply stood and stared as she tried to understand how Dane had grown a full beard in a single hour. He couldn't have, her mind insisted. So it wasn't real.

Right. She stepped forward and yanked at the curling blond hair on his chin.

He yelped in pain, and struck at her hands.

Lorelei let go as suddenly as she'd grabbed him and stepped back against Conan's supporting bulk. "A beard," she whispered, her eyes wide with shock and confusion. "How did you get a beard, Dane?"

The man winked at her. "You may call me Harold," he informed her.

"Harold." The name was as unfamiliar as the man, she realized. "You aren't Dane."

Harold grinned at her. "Certainly I am a Dane. Even if I were not, I might become one to please you."

Dane wasn't Dane, and something was wrong with the universe, Lorelei realized. She'd thought earlier that her confusion was due to some kind of drug. But what if it wasn't? What if it was something else, like, say, time displacement? Or a trip to some kind of alternate universe? There was a parallel reality theory, wasn't there? Some mathematician had written a piece explaining the missing matter problem by some convoluted explanation of probability calculus, which proved that infinite probabilities existed in a "real" state simultaneously. The whole thing had to do with quantum physics and was way beyond her. But what if it wasn't just a theory? What if everything that would ever happen, could happen, or had happened was happening simultaneously and you *could* just step from one probability to another?

Lorelei started to shake.

She grabbed the man she supposed she'd better start calling master by his leather vest and whispered pitifully, "Help."

Erik frowned at her in suspicion. What was the woman about now? Did she expect him to believe she was suddenly overcome with terror at the sight of his brother's beard when she had no fear before a band of Vikings or an Arab slaver?

She frowned back at him and hissed, "Master, all right? Are you happy now? I said it. Now help me, dammit!"

Odd, but her concession did not please him as much as he had expected. He wished her to acknowledge his ownership, true. But she did not seem to really mean it. That was it, he decided. She was humoring him, and he did not find it pleasing to be made the fool in her jesting.

She made a faint noise in her throat, and buried her face in his chest. "Help me, or I'm going to start having a screaming fit right here in front of everyone," she stated in a shaking voice.

He hesitated.

She started to scream.

And scream. And scream. Putting his hand over her mouth only muffled the noise faintly. Erik turned to Harold. "Do something," he grated out. "You upset her with your beard. Make her stop."

Harold put his hands to his face. "I am not going to shave my beard!" he protested, giving Erik a wounded look. "How can you say I upset her? I did nothing."

Svein left his oars and offered helpfully, "When my wife's mother has hysterics, we slap her."

Erik eyed the woman doubtfully. "I do not think that will work."

"Throw water on her," Bjarni suggested.

It was as good an idea as any. Erik nodded, and the men hastily complied. The sound was unnerving. The woman could scream like no other. She made his ears ring and his teeth hurt. He hoped water would work.

Dousing her did prove to have an effect on her, but not necessarily a good one.

She gasped, spluttered, shook her head and wiped at her eyes. She gave him a furious look. Then she started to cry.

The men exchanged helpless looks and retreated to their oars, leaving Erik with a wailing woman in his arms.

He sighed.

Then he picked her up and carried her back to the hold. "Cease," he muttered again, hoping against hope that he might actually be obeyed.

"I can't," she informed him with a sob. She curled her arms around his neck, buried her face against him and continued to weep like one mourning the dead. "I'm lost. I want to go home."

So, she found being his so distressing that she must scream and weep and carry on? His pride wounded, Erik snapped cruelly, "You have no other home. Where I say you belong, you belong. You are my property and you will resign yourself to it and cease these unpleasant displays."

But in contrast to the harsh words, his hands were gentle as he dried her face with a soft linen cloth.

Lorelei sniffed, took it and finished the task, removing the bulk of her stage make-up in the process. Then she took stock of the space the man held her in. Some sort of cargo hold, she supposed, not terribly interested. She had bigger concerns than where they stored their stuff. She dismissed the room, and leaned her cheek against Conan companionably while she tried to sort out everything. And failed.

None of it made sense, and she was tired of thinking about it. For now, she just wanted to let Conan hold her until she felt like coping. She gripped his shoulders in sudden fear, and he looked at her questioningly.

"Don't let go of me," she pleaded. "I might fall into another time warp. Or probability. Or whatever. I don't want to get more lost. Will you just hold onto me?"

Her words were strange, yet Erik thought he understood something of her meaning. She was indeed foreign, and must have been sold into slavery unexpectedly. She was unsure of her place. Unsure of what might befall her next. He slowly let one hand follow the silky raven hair from the crown of her head to her waist. She probably feared he would sell her to another or give her to his men.

He settled her more closely on his lap and held her securely. "I will not let you go," he assured her. "You are mine. Mine alone."

She made a faint choking noise at that. "That's debatable," she muttered. "But we can fight about it later." She shivered and then subsided in his grasp. "Erik, right? That's your name?"

"Yes."

"I'm Lorelei," she offered. Then she shivered again. "This is so insane. We're exchanging names, and next you'll ask me what my sign is. I'm in a cosmic single's bar."

Erik frowned. She was beginning to babble again, and Freya, if she began to scream again he would be sorry he had bought her. Still, she made him curious. "What is this sign?"

"You know, astrology. I'm not a believer. Of course, after today, I might start believing in all sort of things," she answered.

"Do you speak of the stars?"

"Yeah."

He considered that. Then he asked, "Do you mean that you claim to belong to a star? You come from there?"

Lorelei giggled weakly. "No, now you're talking about UFOs. I mean, the star you're born under. Your sign. It's just a conversational opener. Something to say to break the ice."

Erik frowned. She was jesting with him again. "What ice?"

She sighed. "Nothing. Forget it. Let's just not talk for a while, all right?"

No, it was not all right. He pushed her chin up and informed her, "You do not make demands. You will adjust to your new position. You belong to me and you will obey me. Do you understand?"

She understood all right, Lorelei thought wearily. "Put a sock in it," she muttered. "I'm not up to this. You can interrogate me later, can't you? Just think how much more efficient it'll be when I'm not having a nervous breakdown."

"You will not begin to scream again."

"I will not scream again," she parroted. "Especially if you stop asking me questions. If you really want to help, you could give me a drink. I probably really need one." She paused to think that one over. "Then again, maybe getting drunk isn't the answer. It's not going to help me solve this problem."

"We have a saying," Erik returned. "'There is no better load a man can carry than much common sense; no worse a load than too much drink.'"

"Thank you for the Viking proverb," Lorelei muttered dryly.

"You will learn to speak to me with the proper respect."

Lorelei sighed. He had no sense of humor. None at all. The one funny thing he'd said had been totally serious. She had to take a trip into a dimension beyond time and space with Erik the Earnest. It figured.

"So, you're a Viking," she began, deciding that since she couldn't avoid it, she might as well talk about it. Which was when she realized she'd been speaking Algonquin all along. So it really did parallel Old Norse as one disputed language study claimed. Further proof of the Viking settlement in New England. If she ever got home, she could rock the linguistic world. She must have simply responded to the language she heard him speaking without thinking.

"A Dane. Yes," he replied.

"Uh huh." She didn't see that there was any distinction, but she let it ride. "And where are we, Erik?"

That got the literal kind of answer she might have expected. "Aboard my longboat."

"Uh huh."

"What does this mean, 'uh huh'?"

"It means I follow you."

"At last you are beginning to act like a proper slave."

"Not likely," Lorelei grumbled. "But enough about me. Thank you for the information about your boat, but I meant, where are we, geographically speaking?"

"We are leaving Hedeby Noor."

"Uh huh." She let that sink in a moment. Then she asked, "What's Hedeby Noor?"

"The bay Hedeby is located on. You recall Hedeby," he prompted. "I bought you there."

She sat up and gave him a dirty look. "You what? You didn't buy me. I wasn't for sale."

"Yes, you were. And yes, I did. I bought you with hack silver."Lorelei gave him a startled look. "Bought? With hack silver? Are you talking about that coin-chopping bit? Do you mean you paid for me in small change?" Her voice rose sharply on the end of that question, and he frowned at the insolence.

"Hack silver. Not even thirty pieces," she muttered. She subsided into sullen silence for a moment, before grousing, "I'm a bargain basement special. You had to tell me that? I am not impressed."

"You wish I had paid more dearly for you?"

"I wish you hadn't paid for me at all, since that thief had no more right to sell me than you had to buy me. But at least you could have come close to what I'm worth. I have a net that would make your hair curl." Lorelei shot him an indignant look. "I was on the cover of Rolling Stone last month. I haven't left the top ten in two years. And you buy me for a quarter? Oh, the ignominy of it all. I'll never live this one down." When Dane heard about it, he'd really have the story inquiring minds wanted to know, she concluded unhappily. Provided he ever did get to hear about it.

"From where do you come that you are so valued?"

"Hm? Oh, I think you guys called it Vinland. But for all I know you haven't been there yet. What year is it?"

His answer made her groan.

"It can't be, it just can't," she said. "I mean, what else could it be? But how did this happen? One day I'm minding my own business, then wham! I get thrown more than a thousand years into the past? Where's Carl Sagan when you need him?"

Erik's frowned. "You will tell me who this Carl Sagan is," he ordered.

"What?"

"Who is this Carl Sagan? You will answer."

Lorelei sighed. "The one who should be here, seeing this. He's into the cosmos. He'd probably even have an explanation for how this happened. Erik, I don't know how to tell you this, but you just bought a woman from the future."

There was a brief silence.

"You claim that you come from the future?" Erik inquired slowly.

"You got it, handsome." Lorelei patted his chest.

"You will cease to mock me," he stated.

"I mock not," she promised and leaned back against the solid, muscled chest he so thoughtfully provided. "I am from the future. What would you like to know about it? We've got all kinds of stuff you wouldn't believe. We've traveled to the moon. We have satellites and cellular phones. Voice mail. E-mail. We have computers and VCRs and microwaves. In a word, Erik, we have made instant gratification a science."

"Instant gratification?"

Lorelei nodded. "Instant food. Instant information. Instant communication with anyone, anywhere in the world. Zap, your wishes are granted at the touch of a button. We can't do everything. We can't raise the dead, for instance, but we can freeze the terminally ill for future medical breakthroughs."

Erik eyed his prize with sinking sorrow. She was so beautiful. So soft and warm to the touch. True, she had a screech that could make him wish for deafness, but he had had such high hopes, nevertheless.

"I see," he stated gravely. He gently set her away and stood. "I must go see about setting our course," he informed her politely.

"Sure, go ahead." Lorelei dismissed him with a wave.

He backed cautiously out and made his way back on deck. For some time he simply stood, gazing sightlessly at the horizon and feeling the breeze in his face.

"Did you get her to stop her wailing?" Harold teased, coming up beside him.

Erik turned towards him slowly, collecting his thoughts.

"I hear no more sounds," Harold went on. "Did you teach her better things to do with her lips?"

Erik gazed at Harold for a moment. Then he answered. "No, little brother, I did not."

Harold gave him an amazed look. "And why not?"

Erik thought of her claims. That she came from the future. That wishes could be granted. That such things as food could be had instantly, when cooking and hunting took hours. That it was possible to speak with anyone, anywhere, instantly when it took weeks to travel even to the Danelaw and back to exchange messages.

It all added up to one inevitable conclusion. Perhaps she had been a noblewoman sold into slavery. Perhaps she had been born a slave. But whatever her origins, she had been unable to accept the reality of her circumstances.

"Because," Erik stated morosely. "She is—how did she say it? A few bricks shy. Not fully decked. Full of bats. Harold, her wits are addled beyond belief. She is insane."

And, he continued savagely to himself, he could hardly force himself on a witless, defenseless woman. No matter how desirable she might otherwise be.

Chapter Four

Lorelei guessed it was Barney's turn to feed the lunatic.

It was comical, really. The big man practically danced along on his tippy-toes, holding her dinner out as far away from himself as possible, placing it a safe distance from the dangerous madwoman before he practically ran for cover.

As if insanity was contagious.

"Thanks, Barney," she called after his fleeing form. Not that she was particularly hungry. But she did appreciate the thought.

Lorelei lounged back on the luxurious blanket, if that was what it was. Some sort of unusual fur, anyway, in the form of a throw rug or whatever. She frowned in irritation at the reminder that even the most familiar, everyday items were unrecognizable to her. Of course, if the shoe were on the other foot and the Vikings were in her time, they wouldn't even know how to get a drink of water.

There was some comfort in that thought.

Running one hand over the thick, speckled violet fur, Lorelei reflected that at least she had pleasant surroundings. It could have been worse. They could have left her in Heady-whatever to fend for herself. All in all, she had to admit they weren't a bad bunch to get bought or stolen by, if she had to be bought or stolen.

She would really have preferred to go home, though.

On a whim, she raised her legs until they were vertical to the deck, then clicked her emerald sequined heels together three times in midair as she lay on her back, chanting, "There's no place like home. There's no place like home. There's no place like home."

She looked up to see Barney's horrified face frozen above her heels.

"Hi," Lorelei said cheerfully. He already thought she was nuts, so what did it matter if he caught her talking to herself?

The man stared back at her, shocked, then blurted out, "Here is water." He thrust a cup at her before he ran for his life the second time.

Brows raised, Lorelei gazed after him in wonder. Incredible. She had that muscle-bound warrior shaking in his shoes. Or the equivalent of shoes. Whatever the well-dressed Viking wore these days. But no matter what they might be called, Barney was unquestionably quivering in his.

And him with the sword.

Lorelei threw back her head and laughed, then subsided into giggles as she dropped back down to her prior lounging position. It really was funny that she'd managed to intimidate them, but really, it did make some sense. Men were notorious for running for cover in the face of illness. An apparent mental illness just made them run faster. It would seem that human nature remained the same. A man was a man, whatever his age. Or Age.

Lorelei laughed again at her own pun, then drank her water. A little brackish, but then, she wasn't expecting Evian. Whatever its shortcomings, it was cool and wet and soothing to her throat. Her screaming bout had left it raw and aching. The downside to healthy lungs and operatic training; she could scream louder than the average person, but not without consequences. The bread wasn't bad, either .

It felt good to laugh again, and even better to act out the motions of going on with living. After several hours of her own solitary company, she was slowly getting back to some semblance of normality. She was also feeling less on edge as the initial shock faded. Her crying jag had served to anesthetize the worst of her emotional reaction. Still, the whole thing was pretty unnerving. What had happened? And how? A more disturbing question that raised itself was...would it happen again?

That one made her shiver. And sober up.

"Think, Lorelei," she instructed herself firmly. "Things don't just happen." She began to think through the last events she remembered clearly. The rehearsal. Dane teasing her. Getting ready to go onstage for the last concert. And she'd put on the armband. She remembered that.

But where was it now? She wasn't wearing it. If she had been when Erik jumped in with his sword and his small change, he should have noticed it. But he hadn't. So where was it?

The armband was left behind, Dane had said.

She drew her knees up, wrapped her arms around her legs and rested her chin on the convenient point. She was here. The armband wasn't. But it was, in a way. Erik had the identical pair, only they were new. Was one of his the same one Dane had given her? Or was the design a popular one, and the whole thing coincidental?

So much for thinking. With a tired sigh, Lorelei slid back down to curl on the luxurious fur blanket. She had a whole lot of questions to consider, and very few answers. She was also deeply tired, feeling the drain of the demanding tour on her physical and emotional resources as well as the horrible shock of transition she'd experienced when she'd fallen into the past.

"Let that be a lesson to you," she muttered to herself. "Don't accept jewelry from a man. Not even on loan. Make a note of it for future reference."

Not that she was likely to forget.

On deck, it sounded like the men were done working for the day. Voices raised in banter mingled with the continual roar of the surf and the wind. Funny how noisy a sailboat was. Lorelei listened to the rhythm of the wind and wave, the water slapping against the longboat's prow and unconsciously began to tap a counter rhythm with her fingertips. Lying there, alone, listening, she thought she could almost feel the rhythm of a different time. The male voices made a counterpoint to the sounds of nature. They fit. This was their place. Their time.

And she was the alien. Even her heart beat out of syncopation.

It was a long time before she fell asleep. Once she did, she slept uneasily, dreaming a series of repeating images. Dane, holding the armband, with tears in his eyes. A black void. A gold and silver circle that was laid out like a flowing Moebius strip, twining and turning across a silent night sky. Lorelei ran after it, and when she caught it, it turned on her and became a clawing, hissing beast.

Harold clouted Bjarni affectionately and passed him the mead. "Drink, friend," he urged. "You look as pale as a Saxon."

Bjarni frowned at the insult, but drank anyway. "If I am pale, that slave woman is the cause. She laughed. Did you hear? I tell you, it gave me the chills. The sound of her mad laughter is as bad as her shrieking."

Erik watched the two distantly and wished they would speak of something else. He found the reminder of the dark woman he'd brought on board most unwelcome. What had come over him, that he had suddenly believed he must have her at any cost? He must have been possessed by evil spirits. She was surely Loki's daughter come to trouble him.

A wise man would sell her, and quickly. To another lusting fool who would see only her beauty.

Yet...she had looked so small, so helpless, clinging to him with tears in her eyes. She was his. She had turned to him for comfort.

Yes, she was his. His property. An investment, nothing more. And a poor one, at that, Erik decided. Her beauty had no doubt turned other foolish heads and caused former owners to spoil her, encouraging her to believe her value to be greater than it was. She was good for a man's pleasure and no more. She had no skills and no strength to labor at any hard task. He scowled, thinking of it. Of her. Of his own foolishness.

He should sell her and be rid of her. Then he would be rid of the evidence of his foolish actions and free also of the twisted desire he felt for one so blighted.

Erik considered that while he checked the sun's position and angle with his sunstone, then searched out Polaris. The star was dimly visible in the extended northern daylight. From these sightings and from countless other cues he read nearly automatically after years of familiarity with the sea, he found the longboat's position and adjusted their course.

He could easily stop and sell the woman before they neared home. If he sold her, he wanted never to lay eyes on her again. It was better to do it far from home.

Better, because a fire of rage burned in him at the thought of another having her.

Bjarni's voice broke through his thoughts then. "I tell you, she can starve before I take food to her again," the man grumbled.

Harold laughed. "She is only a woman, Bjarni. What matter if she has the mind of a child? She has the body of a woman!

My brother has the best of it with his new slave. But if you are afraid of her, I will see to her on the morrow." The sexual meaning in his voice and his teasing wink were not unnoticed by Erik.

"You will 'see' to her food and drink only," he snapped, holding Harold's eyes directly as he spoke.

"Yes, certainly, brother," Harold returned innocently. "What else would I do?"

Erik hesitated, then decided it was not worth pursuing. Instead he dismissed him with a nod and settled down for the night.

Without conscious thought, his eyes turned towards the place his slave slept. Realizing what he was doing, he turned away with a dark scowl.

He would not think of her.

He would not care if she still cried and wanted to go home.

He would not wonder if she had eaten or not.

Would he not? Erik sighed inwardly and rolled onto his back to look up at the sky. He thought of nothing else. She was a curse.

When Harold took out his pan flute and began to play softly, he concentrated on that until he fell asleep.

"Good morning."

The cheerful masculine voice broke through the last hazy remnant of an uneasy dream and Lorelei blinked awake. Her gaze wandered around the odd cabin until they came to rest on the man who looked like Dane but wasn't. He was grinning broadly at her, mischief alive in his eyes.

Lorelei smiled back unconsciously. He was so like Dane. And he was up to no good. "Good morning. Aren't you afraid of the dangerous madwoman?"

Harold winked. "What should I fear? That you will steal my heart? I thought you were mad, not a thief. Perhaps I am safe enough. What do you think?"

Lorelei tipped her head to one side and considered him mock-seriously. "Hm. Well, I'm a bit tired just now and your heart looks like it wouldn't be easy to get to. I guess you're safe. Especially if you brought coffee. Do you guys have coffee?"

The grinning blond walked over to sit beside her on the fur and offered her more water and bread. "What is coffee?"

Lorelei sighed in resignation. "Out of my reach, at the moment. It's made from a kind of ground beans. It's sort of bitter at first, but it's a stimulant. It makes you wake up. It even makes waking up kind of enjoyable."

When was coffee discovered? Not until sometime after the fourteenth or fifteenth century at least, if she remembered right. Although she wasn't a historian. Which meant she wouldn't be getting any for at least six hundred years. A Starbucks Caramel Macchiato was even further out of reach in the distant future. Since residents of Seattle considered their daily latte nearly a constitutional right, it was painful to realize she couldn't even get a cup of instant Folger's

"Where does this bean grow?" Harold asked, curious.

"South America, mostly, I think. Tropical places. Mountainous areas near the equator—ah, where it doesn't snow," Lorelei explained quickly. "But I'm guessing, Harold. I get it from, oh, a local merchant, I guess you'd say. I don't go buy it from the source myself and I never really gave it much thought before."

She'd never given quite a few things much thought before, Lorelei admitted silently. How was she supposed to prove anything she said? She didn't know how to do anything that would impress these guys, like build an electric generator.

"Tell me something else about your home," Harold suggested.

She considered him over the rim of her cup. "What do you want to know?"

"Where is it?"

She laughed and drank the water in one long swallow before answering. "A long ways away from here. Vikings settled in Iceland and Greenland after a king took over and unified the Norsemen—"

"What? One king?" The startled interruption broke through her explanation.

"Oh, not for a long time, yet," she assured him. "But for obvious reasons, a lot of the nobles decided it was time to move on. So they colonized Greenland, then Iceland. Then they settled in Vinland from there. That's where I live. Or lived, anyway." Suddenly depressed at the reminder of her lost home, Lorelei drew her knees up and rested her cheek on them.

"This Vinland where there is coffee, you could find it again?" the blond asked her nonchalantly, but the intensity in his eyes gave him away.

Lorelei shook her head. "You don't have any better a poker face than Dane does." She sighed. "That's why I always beat him. Harold, I couldn't even get you from here to the North Pole. I don't know where here is, and even if I did, I don't exactly have any landmarks to go by."

His disappointment was so plain she almost laughed.

"Sorry," she offered, with a pat on the shoulder. "There go your dreams of exploration and great discoveries."

Her laughing eyes fell on a small set of pipes he carried. Some kind of musical instrument? It wasn't anything she recognized. "What's that?"

In answer, he put it to his mouth and played a soft note.

"A flute of some kind?" Eagerly, she held out a hand and Harold gave it to her. She turned it over, examining it. "Hey, neat! It looks like a pan flute, but I've never seen one this small." Experimentally, she put her lips to it and blew. The clear sound made her smile in delight. Then she played a rapid series of notes, closing her eyes to hear more clearly the unique sound the pan flute made.

"This is great, Harold!" she enthused. "Jethro Tull would love this."

Still smiling, she handed it back.

Harold eyed her thoughtfully. "You know how to play it," he stated.

"Sure. I learned how to play all kinds of things. Even the toy piano. You never know what sound you might need for a song," Lorelei explained. "I can keep time on a drum, although it isn't what I'm best at, and I'm okay on the guitar. Do you have one of those?"

A guitar would be a gift from heaven. If she was going to be some kind of captive, she could at least entertain herself and keep her sanity by working on some new material.

She was certainly surrounded by enough raw ideas. She could do a whole album on her current circumstances, Lorelei thought wryly. She could just picture it. Paul Simon did a collaboration with South African musicians. She could work with musicians from the ancient world. It would certainly be unique. And what a follow-up to her last album. She could get Thor's Hammer to collaborate.

Sure, she could. All she had to do was figure out how to undo whatever she'd done so she could go back to her own time. Piece of cake.

Harold was still giving her a funny look. "A guitar."

"Do you have a different word for it? A wooden box, hollow, with a neck. Strings made from very thin metal or gut go across an opening on the hollow box to the top of the neck." With her hands she pantomimed the shape and size. "You strum it. Do you know what I mean?"

Harold nodded slowly. "Yes, I do. I have one, but not here."

Lorelei sighed. "I should have known. The damp sea air probably isn't very good for wooden instruments. Well, thanks anyway."

The bearded man studied her intently for a moment. "What did you say to my brother to make him believe you were mad?"

"Oh, not much. I told him I came from the future."

"From the future."

"Yeah, that I traveled back in time hundreds of years."

"Hundreds of years?"

"Hundreds."

"And you described to him this future you came from?"

"Yeah. Probably a bad idea, huh?"

Harold smiled his crooked, devilish smile. Then he threw back his head and roared with laughter. "A bad idea? No, no. A very good idea. Very bold and clever, too. My brother had better watch his back."

Lorelei eyed him guardedly, and he winked at her. "You have no need to worry. If he wishes to think you mad, we will let him, eh?" He laughed again, then stood. "Much as I might wish otherwise, I am not free to spend the day in your pleasant company. You may keep this, however." He tossed the miniature flute to her and she caught it reflexively.

"Thanks." She flashed him a smile, delighted to have something to amuse herself with.

Harold shook his head slightly as if bewildered. "No, I should thank you. Because of you, this dull voyage has become most interesting." He started to go, then turned back as if overcome by curiosity. "What did it feel like to travel on the sea of time?"

"Imagine being turned inside out. Then imagine being horribly seasick," Lorelei suggested wryly.

Harold laughed again at her reply. "You tell the most interesting stories." Still laughing, the blond man strode away, probably to go back to rowing, Lorelei supposed. What did Vikings do all day on a longboat? She had no idea. Then she thought about his words and smiled.

Told interesting stories, did she? Yes, from where he stood they had to sound like tall tales, although her mention of a product he was unfamiliar with and places he hadn't heard of had caught his attention. Harold was certainly a guy with an ear to the ground looking for opportunity. Interesting that he'd ignored mention of time travel and the future of the Vikings to zero in on a new area of trade to exploit. Practical, these Vikings. That is, if he was typical of the breed.

Too bad she hadn't ever bothered to learn much about the culture. The odd facts she did remember were things she'd picked up accidentally while learning something related. Norse mythology, for example. The language study documenting the parallel between Old Norse and Algonquin. The Viking settlement in America. That was about the extent of her knowledge, except that she thought they were known for surprise attacks on seaside towns and villages.

Wonderful. She was in a time she didn't even know the cultural norms or values of. Important things like, how did they treat women? On the one hand, she'd been grabbed, bought at sword-point, which basically left the seller no choice, and stashed aboard ship. On the other hand, she'd been treated decently in spite of her raving hysteria.

She did know something, though. Harold obviously believed her to be a conniving liar, and he'd enjoyed her company and given her his flute to play with. What could she make of that? That maybe lying was a respected skill? She thought of Native

American customs involving gift-giving, and realized that she had better tread carefully until she knew what an action like that meant.

She'd better watch her step, period. She couldn't take even the smallest things for granted. She was in an alien culture. A real stranger in a strange land. And without a guide.

Lorelei mused soberly that maybe giving them the impression she was out of her mind was the best thing that could have happened. They wouldn't expect sane behavior from her. As it was, from what her "master" had said, she was already in trouble and deserved some sort of punishment.

She grinned in pure mischief, thinking of various ways to keep up the appearance of a crazy woman. If she didn't get herself killed, she might even get to have some fun. And why not? She was due for a vacation. True, she'd originally planned to spend it around Puget Sound, not Hedeby Noor. But a vacation was a vacation. And how many people got the opportunity for a vacation from their whole life?

People paid good money to go participate in mystery vacations, acting out assigned parts in the drama and trying to outwit the "criminal". The idea of stepping outside of one's own life and limitations had universal appeal. For the famous, going unnoticed was hard to manage outside of Mardi Gras. And here she was, dropped into a character role out of the blue without fear of a mob scene. She wouldn't be recognized because she was only a legend in her *own* time. Here, she was just Lorelei. Crazy slave, to Erik and the rest of the crew. Fabulous liar, to Harold. And to herself?

To herself, Lorelei realized, she was just what she'd always been. A woman. A musician. And now, a woman musician on a unique kind of vacation.

She was also a woman in need of something to wear. The green dry-clean only dress wasn't made for the abuse of wrestling, sword-fighting, and rescuing, although as it turned out it hadn't been a rescue after all. Followed by a dunking in sea water. Then she'd added insult to the multiple injuries the delicate fabric had already sustained by sleeping in it.

Lorelei examined the stained and torn dress critically and considered her options.

Maybe she could talk to Harold about her clothing crisis.

Maybe "master Erik" could be shamed into doing something about it. After all, if he was responsible for her, he should take care of her little problem. Shouldn't he?

Although she had to admit, her present appearance did a lot to uphold her image as resident nutcase. All she needed was a shopping bag to complete the ensemble.

Giggling at the mental picture of herself posing as a bag lady superimposed over the glamorous Rolling Stone cover, Lorelei slipped out of her shoes and discarded her stockings. To her disbelief, they hadn't run. Now there was a celebrity endorsement story. Too bad nobody would ever believe it. But she made a mental note to buy stock in the company if—no, she corrected herself firmly, *when* she got home.

Except for her hair, she was about as cleaned up as she could get. A search through the cabin uncovered a carved comb and she made use of it, grimacing at the snarls in her long hair.

It occurred to her that the biggest difference she saw between her own time and this one was the pre-Industrial Revolution manufacturing. Everything was handmade. So everything was unique. And the makers apparently were artists. She turned the comb over in her hand, examining it carefully. It was beautiful, decorated with whorls and loops like the pattern on Barney's sword. How long did it take to carve a comb like this? And what was its value? Did the items stored with her represent luxuries, or were they the norm?

"More questions you don't have answers to," she sighed out loud, frustrated.

Well, if she was going to cope, she'd have to be watchful and aware to pick up on whatever clues she got about the Norse psyche. Since she had no way of telling how long she'd be there, it seemed smart to make some kind of place for herself. For all she knew, being Erik's private property was a desirable position. Time would tell. But if it wasn't, she should look for options.

Meanwhile, she should stay busy, and a workout would help her nerves. Lorelei stood easily, balanced, and began controlled breathing as she flowed slowly through a series of tai chi movements. The very slow exercises required deceptive strength and muscle control to perform correctly. She hadn't been doing it long enough to have any kind of mastery, but her instructor had started to say kind things recently.

Moving from Grasp Sparrow's Tail to Ward Off, Lorelei reflected that her self-defense training might come in handy soon. She should take the exercise more seriously now. Although the twentieth century wasn't necessarily any less dangerous. After a female musician's murder in Seattle, she'd made sure the other Sirens took some kind of training, too. None of them would be helpless victims if she had anything to say about it. They'd have a fighting chance in a do-or-die situation.

For Lorelei, fighting for the life she wanted wasn't anything new. She might be out of her element, but she was still a fighter. Talent, intelligence and determination had always kept her going. She'd found a way to succeed in the highly competitive, demanding profession she'd chosen. She'd find a way to make it here, too.

Determination fueled her tiring muscles through the final graceful movement. Then she sank down to rest and catch her breath, relieved and pleased at the proof that she was really all right.

Her heart still beat. Her lungs still pumped air. Her muscles still moved and flexed on demand.

Not bad for a woman eleven hundred years from her own time.

Chapter Five

By the time Harold came back, Lorelei was fed up with her own company and the four walls around her. She practically pounced on the man, as eager for the sight and sound of another human being as for the water he brought.

"Harold! Great to see you. Listen, I've got a few questions you might be able to answer."

Her enthusiastic opener drew an answering smile from her accomplice. "What questions are those?"

She beamed at the helpful response, took his arm and led him to the fur blanket she'd taken to sitting on since there didn't seem to be any chairs. He handed her the carved cup and she took it gladly. "Thanks. Well, for starters, Harold, am I a prisoner? Can I walk around?"

The bearded man regarded her thoughtfully. "Erik did not say you were not allowed to move about freely."

"So, if he didn't say it, I'm not held to it? Good. Because I have to tell you, Harold, I have one bad case of cabin fever. I don't think I can stay in here another hour." Lorelei paused to drink the water, set the cup aside and went on. "There's also a little problem you might be able to shed some light on."

Harold blinked. "You need more light?"

"What? Oh, no, the sun never seems to go down. It's like Alaska in the summertime. There's plenty of light, Harold. I meant in an informational sense." She leaned confidentially towards him. "Harold, I don't have any clothes."

To her amazement, he blushed. Actually blushed. Although his face was so reddened from the sun already that she hadn't thought it could darken further. She hesitated briefly. Was this a no-no to talk about? Was she embarrassing him? Well, maybe, but they'd all be really embarrassed if she didn't get some more clothes. And quickly. Since she'd already brought it up, Lorelei decided, she might as well keep going.

"I was wondering if you could tell me what I could do about getting something to wear."

Harold blushed redder. "You, ah, uh, you...that is, if you please your, ah..." he trailed off in embarrassment, cleared his throat and fell silent for a moment. Finally, he asked, "What did you do among your people when you had need of something?"

"Well, I write and sing songs."

He nodded slowly. "As I thought. You are a skald. If you are good, you are given gifts and coins?"

Lots of coins. He had no idea. Gifts, too, although she hadn't really thought about it. She did get some extravagant presents from her manager, fans, the record company. The perks made up for the inconveniences of being well-known. "Yeah, Harold, I think it's safe to say I'm given a lot of gifts and coins."

He nodded again. "So. You will sing for me, and I will give you a gown. A bargain?"

"Sure thing." She held out her hand to shake on it, and after a pause, Harold clumsily took her hand but seemed to have no idea what to do with it. "We'll shake on the deal. Like this." She demonstrated.

"Oh. I see." Harold pumped her hand in return. "This means we are agreed? We have a bargain?"

She winked at him. "We do. Now, what kind of song would you like? No, don't tell me, let me guess. I'm good at this. I was a street musician for a few months, you know. You get good at knowing what to sing for who when continuing to eat is at stake." Lorelei eyed Harold and thought about what she knew of him. He liked travel and adventure. Probably wine, women and song, too.

She sang him Janis Joplin's version of Bobbie McGee, in English since it wouldn't rhyme in translation. Besides, her brief flirtation with opera had taught her that language didn't matter if the musician communicated the emotion of a song; the audience would hear and understand.

She knew how to make an audience understand.

By the time she'd sung it through, Harold had tears in his eyes. He caught her hands in a crushing grip. "Stop. That is enough. You will get the finest gown I can give you." He stood and went to a bale of goods in one corner. The gown he retrieved was green silk shot through with silver thread.

"Hey, wow! This is gorgeous, Harold. Really, really beautiful. I have a Dior original that isn't this beautiful. It's perfect." She kissed his bearded cheek and skipped behind piles of stuff to change. She tossed her sadly abused outfit out behind her and shimmied into the silk dress. Then her smile faded and died as she looked in vain for a zipper, a button, a hook. Anything. The gown opened at the shoulder and didn't seem to close.

Great. She had new clothes, and she was still indecent. She thought it might fit tightly enough to stay up, but she wouldn't count on it. She sighed.

Clutching the top together, she stuck her head out and peered around at Harold. "Uh, I have another problem."

He didn't seem surprised.

"The dress. Um, it won't stay up. Closed. On," Lorelei elaborated.

"Hm." Harold stroked his beard as if contemplating the problem, but the wicked gleam in his eyes gave him away.

"All right, now what?" Lorelei demanded, stalking back out with one hand holding the fabric together.

"Hm. A problem, you say? I see no problem."

Lorelei sighed. "You're an extortionist. But I'm at your mercy. Okay, what do you want for a button?"

"Another song."

She frowned at him. "No funny stuff. If you give me a button, that has to include the means to put it on. No tricks." She wasn't going to keep singing for a needle, then thread. At least, not without trying for a better deal first.

He looked slightly confused. "Button is the same as pin, is it not? You want something to fasten your gown?"

"Yeah, wise guy, I want something to fasten my gown. Okay, I'll sing you another song." She'd sing him a song to make him sorry he'd pulled a fast one. She knew how to manipulate an audience's emotions and push buttons. She could stir him up, make him squirm and leave him hanging. And she would.

She did.

Five minutes later, he was pinning her gown together at the shoulder with a circular silver brooch. His hands were shaking, but he was true to his promise to get her dressed. Lorelei watched him stop, start over and nearly drop the pin in his state. Maybe it hadn't been fair of her to vamp it up like that. She winced in sympathy when he jabbed himself in the finger once. But overall, she was feeling too pleased with herself to repent.

The pin was a beauty, too. The now-familiar animal motif with curlicues she was beginning to recognize as a common theme in Viking decoration resembled a stylized wolf. It complemented the green and silver dress wonderfully. As if the dress needed any help to be a knockout. Tight sleeves and a tightly fitted bodice molded her curves above the skirt that fell straight to the floor. The style was made to flatter women. Something the twentieth century designers seemed to forget, in Lorelei's opinion.

When Harold finished, she beamed at him. "Thanks. You're a darling."

"And you are going to become very wealthy, if Erik does not kill you first."

"Now, why would he want to do that?"

"Why, indeed," Harold muttered. "He may simply decide to kill the rest of us, instead."

Lorelei grinned at him. "Don't be such a pessimist. I thought you were bored. I thought you were looking forward to having things livened up a little."

"True." He grinned back at her.

"Well, then, let's go strut our stuff." Lorelei placed a hand on his arm and dropped one lid in a wink. "Lead on. I believe you know the way. And maybe you could tell me a little bit about our fearless leader while you're at it."

"You wish to know about Erik?"

Oh, yes, she did. Not only did finding out everything she could about the man who currently held her fate in his hands seem smart, she was curious. He intrigued her. If they'd met under different circumstances, she would have been interested enough to want to get to know him better. And, well, he was riveting. Not just gorgeous. He commanded attention and radiated strength. The combination was almost lethally sexy.

Out loud, she simply said, "You betcha. I wish to know lots of things, but let's start with the big ones and work down. Like, why am I here?"

"Why are you here?"

Lorelei stopped and frowned at Harold impatiently. "Is there an echo in here? Come on, Harold. Why grab me out of all the choices open to the enterprising Viking with a sword? Let's face it, I didn't make a good first impression if he had a job opening for a malleable, obedient slave girl."

Harold hesitated. Then he said slowly, "I think Erik himself knows not why you are here."

"But you do?" Lorelei prompted.

On the point of answering, he was rudely cut off by the subject of their conversation himself.

There he was again, larger than life and twice as determined, Lorelei mused. And in an outfit that could give even the most conservative woman a leather fetish. What that body of his did for chaps...although they weren't chaps, exactly. More like suede pants with leather thong ties. Whatever, the total effect had her mesmerized. Until his words penetrated the haze of instant lust surrounding her brain.

"You will explain and you will begin now," he grated out, advancing on Harold with unspoken menace, "and you will begin with why you have your hand on her, and why she wears the gown you bought for Gudred."

Lorelei shot Harold a dirty look. "You gave me some other woman's clothes? Thanks a lot."

Both men ignored her. Harold gave Erik a sly smile. "I gave her the dress as a gift. She pleased me more than Gudred."

Erik's fist erased the smile.

Lorelei fell back automatically and watched in disbelief as the two men proceeded to exchange blows over the state of her wardrobe. Maybe she shouldn't have asked Harold about clothes. Maybe it had been a mistake not to take it up with Erik first. Maybe some matter of honor or pride was at stake.

Or maybe they were just nuts.

"Hey, enough already!" She caught Erik's arm and glared at him. "If you're offended, that's too bad, but you should have done something about it yourself. You had time." The caustic reminder might have been a little too rude. His eyes took on a particularly icy shade of blue and for a minute she thought she really might have something to fear from him.

He took her arm in a death grip and snarled, "There is no time like the present."

"Well, thanks, but no thanks, buddy. You're a little late now. Your brother already took care of it," Lorelei pointed out. Although on the other hand, maybe she ought to take him up on his sudden interest in her needs. One new dress wouldn't get her far, and she might be stuck here for a long time. "On second thought, maybe I can do a repeat performance."

The grip tightened and Lorelei gasped, more in indignation than pain. "Ouch! Let go, you jerk!"

He didn't let go. He started towards the shelter she'd just left, taking her arm with him and leaving her no choice but to follow along. "Cut it out! You're going to leave a bruise if you don't let up!"

He adjusted his grip but otherwise gave no indication that he'd heard a word she said. Lorelei supposed she should be grateful for small favors, but as he continued dragging her back to the cabin, she didn't see much to be grateful for. She'd just gotten out. If he wanted her back indoors, she wasn't going to cooperate. She deliberately dragged her feet and forced him to carry her full weight in silent protest.

Being silent didn't sit well with her, though.

"You're acting like a barbarian," she ground out between clenched teeth, in case his behavior had escaped his notice. "You can't just haul me around like this."

"I can do whatever I wish with you."

The cold, grim voice hit right on her aggravation button and she'd already had enough to keep her in a fighting mood for a week even without the choice of words.

"Wrong," she snapped.

When he didn't answer she planted her feet and leaned back until he looked at her. "Answer me when I'm fighting with you, buster."

He looked faintly incredulous.

"You demand I fight you?"

It was kind of ridiculous, put like that. Lorelei felt her anger evaporating, and humor twitched at the corner of her mouth.

"I guess it is kind of funny," she admitted. Then she giggled. The giggles grew to full laughter at the disbelief in his eyes. She had demanded, actually demanded, that this overgrown behemoth fight her. It was too absurd. She laughed until her side ached, and then slumped against him, panting, while she recovered. She didn't even protest when he finished hauling her back to her now-familiar fur.

Or when he threw her down on it and followed suit himself.

Until the grim look in his eye combined with the grip on the contested dress told her where he was headed.

She froze. Her mind was racing a million miles an hour, but her body was frozen like a deer caught in the oncoming headlights of a semi. She'd been the focus of plenty of masculine attention. But she'd never been on the receiving end of anything like this. He looked like a conquering hero bent on taking what he wanted, and he wanted her. Some dark part of her stirred to life and wondered what it would be like to be taken sexually by this man. To be seized and captured and overpowered.

Maybe she was about to find out. One thing she knew for certain, she was fully aware of him. He had her attention in a way no other man had ever managed. She knew the feminine awareness and dark curiosity showed in her eyes and she didn't care. She waited, unable to do anything else, and wondered what he would do next.

She wasn't afraid of him, exactly, although there was a certain amount of fear and it added an erotic edge to the moment. But underneath that was something else. From the beginning she'd stood up to him without hesitation. Why? Because she was used to calling the shots? Or because on an instinctual level she knew he could be trusted?

The answer came instantly. Because he could be trusted.

He might consider her his to possess, but she didn't really believe he would hurt her. Although she couldn't be sure of anything, and that uncertainty mixed with the sexually charged tension between them and ignited it.

His face was expressionless, but his eyes were burning as they held hers. He unfastened her pin with unhurried hands and set it aside. And then he lifted her slightly and stripped the gown from her in one fluid motion, leaving her naked and exposed.

But his eyes remained on hers and she held his gaze. *Fascination.* That was the only word for this. She was utterly focused on him, captivated by him, his captive both in her mind and her unexpected physical response. In that moment, she didn't think she could or would resist anything he wanted of her.

For countless, endless seconds, or maybe hours, there was silence.

Then he spoke.

"I am your master. You will remember that. And you will wear no other man's gifts."

She went cold with shock at that revealing command. "I will wear...what? Do you mean this whole scene is over what I wear?"

Not because he'd wanted her, not because he'd been caught up in the same strange obsession that had overtaken her brain. That hurt. And the hurt turned to anger in self-defense. Fury returned in full force and edged out the uncomfortable and unexpected vulnerability.

"You dragged me in here over that? Because your brother felt sorry for me and gave me something to wear when you obviously didn't care enough to see to it yourself?"

She was so angry, she actually fell speechless for a minute. She closed her eyes to recover. When she had a partial grip on herself, she bit out, "Get off of me and get out of my sight."

"I am not in your sight. Your eyes are shut."

"Do you always have to be so damn literal?" Lorelei demanded.

"So what?" He frowned at the unfamiliar words.

"Literal. It means you take everything seriously, which is a very annoying trait. I'm not very happy with you right now, Erik, and if you don't want a real fight on your hands, you'll take your overgrown self elsewhere. Quickly."

"I care not if you are happy with me," he answered.

"That's obvious." Lorelei opened her eyes to glare at him more effectively. "If you were interested in my happiness, you would think of little things like the fact that I have nothing to wear and that I need some fresh air and sunshine at least every few days." Her sarcasm didn't carom off of his thick skull that time, however.

He frowned, the picture of Barbarian the Perplexed. "You had nothing to wear? You needed air?"

"Right the first time. Give the boy a prize." She shot sparks at him from her eyes. "If you want a pet, Junior, you had better learn to take care of it yourself."

The insults were clear from her tone, even if the words were hard to understand. But Erik let her impudence go without a reprimand. In truth, she had the right of it. He had neglected her and shirked his duty, and all because he did not wish to be reminded of his error in taking her to begin with. And so his error was compounded. If he heard her aright, Harold had only done as he asked, seen to her needs. Not used her to satisfy his own.

He had read his own guilt in his brother's face. He wanted her beyond reason, and so he must believe all other men did as well. Although he found it difficult to believe any man could hear her sing like that and remain unaffected. It still pricked at him that she had chosen to sing for his brother and not for him. But then, had he given her any opportunity? He had avoided her and she was not to blame for his neglect or his jealousy. Or for his idiocy in not recognizing sooner that she was as sound of mind as he was himself.

Truthfully, he had wished to believe her mad. He had grasped at the excuse to distance himself from her and from his unaccountable response to her. But no man or woman could have such skill with music and be lacking in wits.

Silently, he sat up and gathered her into his arms in a wordless attempt to make amends.

Lorelei recognized an olive branch when she saw one. There wasn't any point in refusing to accept the gesture. In fact, she'd be a real prize idiot to turn down any cooperation she was fortunate enough to find. So she rested her cheek on Erik's broad chest and accepted his silent apology, which was probably the closest thing she could expect to get from him, considering.

She reminded herself that she couldn't expect him to act according to her values. He came from another time. Another culture. And by his standards, he'd probably been more than fair in his treatment of her. Still, she couldn't help being a product of her own time any more than he could. She'd fight for every concession she could conceivably win.

Her quirky sense of humor asserted itself, and it dawned on her that she made every bit as terrible a slave as he made a master. The realization went a long ways towards enabling her to feel forgiving.

Lorelei curled in his lap, feeling oddly as safe and protected with him now as she had when he'd first stepped in to rescue her, in spite of the sexual threat he'd posed moments before. It was weird, but she didn't feel uncomfortable being naked with him. The light pressure of his lips grazing her temple added to the sensation of being somehow cherished. She wasn't sure, but she thought the salute was meant as another peace offering, and an assurance of good faith.

In answer, she slipped her arms around his waist. Then she sighed. "Erik, do you think we'll ever be able to get along?"

"Get along?"

"Yes. You know. Get along. Not fight."

"Certainly we will 'get along'." Assurance rang in his authoritative reply. "You will learn to obey, and there will be no more argument."

She half-groaned, half-laughed at that. "Somehow, Erik, I don't think it's going to be anywhere near that simple."

She felt him stroke the length of her hair before he tipped her chin up to study her face. "You are mine. What could be more simple than that?" The question was evidently a rhetorical one, since he didn't wait for an answer. Instead, he lowered his lips to hers in a mind-bending kiss.

She felt the jolt of awareness all the way down to her center of gravity as his mouth moved over hers, searing her with his heat. When he raised his head, she actually thought he'd branded the imprint of his lips on hers. One hand flew to her mouth to trace the imprint as her dazed eyes met his.

"Why did you do that?" The stupid question escaped Lorelei before she could stop it, but she was too shocked to think.

"I did that because I wished to."

The answer wasn't exactly reassuring.

Neither was his next statement.

"Tonight I will do all that I wish with you."

She sputtered at that. "You what? You...you..." Words failed and she ground to a halt. Because her imagination was painting an intensely erotic, vivid picture of all that he might wish to do to her. And some formerly unsuspected dark part of her was riveted. The brief sensation of being in his power sexually had given her a taste of what might happen and just how much she might like it. And that alarmed her. She had a previously unimagined vulnerability that he could exploit until she was his willing slave by her own desire as well as by his archaic laws.

She shoved that possibility away with a fierce will. Unacceptable. She had too much pride to be his plaything. And now she was in the exasperating position of having to resist her own weakness as well as him.

"You heard me not? Tonight I will take you as I please."

She practically gnashed her teeth. Get along, would they? Not likely. "I heard you just fine. I'm not deaf. Erik, you can't just..." Lorelei broke off in frustration as she realized that as far as he was concerned, he could. He actually thought he could do exactly as he pleased. He thought he owned her. And some treacherous, traitorous part of her found that exciting. What was wrong with her? First he had her developing a leather fetish and now fantasies of forced seduction? After a lifetime of celibacy she was suddenly hot for a man who thought she was his love slave?

He was making her insane. That was the only explanation.

Okay, so she couldn't reason with herself. She couldn't reason with him. What did that leave? She could play for time. She did at least have until tonight, that was something.

"Fine," she snarled. "Then meanwhile, why don't you find something else for me to wear and take me back out to get some air before I smother and die in here and deprive you of your fun."

In a huff, she moved off his lap and curled her arms around her legs to prevent him from looking at her. She wasn't giving him any cheap thrills, or any reason to rearrange his schedule, either.

"These demands must cease. No woman who talks as much as you can be in danger of suffocating. You will stay here, and you will stay as I leave you. If I wish you to dress, I will give you clothing to cover yourself with."

With that arrogant reply, he left her sitting there, naked and indignant.

Lorelei stared after his broad departing back in disbelief. Then she yelled after him, "I don't get any clothes? What am I supposed to do in the winter?"

He ignored that question, and Lorelei found that very unsettling.

She thought she remembered that winter in the extreme north got awfully cold.

"If I get frostbite, I'll sue you!" she shouted in defiance.

Then she eyed the thick fur and hoped that wherever she ended up, she had plenty of them around.

Chapter Six

Since she had the opportunity, Lorelei decided she might as well indulge in the once-in-a-lifetime opportunity to sprawl on a luxurious fur wearing only her skin. It was an unbelievably sensual experience. The thick, silky fur stroked and caressed her and she cuddled in the welcoming folds.

"Now that you're comfortable, it's time to start using that brain of yours," she announced. "You haven't exactly been acting like you're playing with a full deck."

Great. And now she was talking to herself.

Well, whatever worked. She'd go with it. She didn't have anyone else around to bounce ideas off of. An unusual experience, for her. How often was she ever really alone? Forget the crowded conditions on the road. At home, it was the same. She even shared a house with the rest of the band. They'd started out that way to save money in the early days, but the advantages quickly became evident to all of the Sirens.

Living together, they could always find each other to run through an idea or work out a variation for a part. It saved time they would have spent traveling to rehearsals and moving equipment from home to practice sessions. With a studio in the house, working at home came naturally. They had a lot more money now, but it just meant a bigger house and better equipment. What had started as financial necessity was now a matter of preference and convenience.

None of the band members were married. Sara had been the exception, and her replacement was single. Lorelei realized that she hadn't been without a close support group for years. No wonder she was so off kilter now. Not having the people she was used to depending on, getting lost in time. Anybody would be thinking a little slowly if they found themselves in her shoes.

Still, the brain set people apart from the animals. Brains went a lot further than brute strength. Since she was clearly outclassed in the brute strength category, she had only her brain to fall back on.

That being the case, she had better start using it.

Now, what did she know about Erik? First of all, he'd taken a very strong interest in her or he wouldn't have bothered to make a scene in the marketplace over a mere slave. And he'd apparently lost interest when she gave him reason to believe she was deranged. But now he'd changed his mind. Why?

Something had changed his mind. Something like Harold spending time with her? Lorelei considered that, turning it over mentally. No. Not enough. He'd dragged her in here and torn off her clothes out of...jealousy.

Now that she was putting two and two together, she realized he'd thought she'd performed an age-old service in exchange for the gown.

Not very flattering to realize the opinion he held of her, but then he didn't know her. She wouldn't prostitute herself. She'd go naked and starve first. In fact, she'd gotten awfully skinny a few times early on in her career. If she hadn't been desperate enough on the streets of Seattle, she wouldn't be now.

Given the attraction between them and adding the touchy subject of her slave status, she could understand his possessiveness. But he could have just explained.

No, Lorelei reasoned further, he couldn't have. First of all, it would never have occurred to him that she didn't understand the culture. He didn't believe her time-travel story anymore than Harold did. So why would he explain? Further, why should he explain anything to a slave? She didn't know the Viking attitude towards slavery, but in most societies, slaves weren't treated with a lot of courtesy.

"Erik, you're a very fortunate Viking," she decided out loud. "If I hadn't spent so much time listening to oral traditions and studying myths and legends from other cultures, I wouldn't be nearly as sympathetic to you as I am. And you would need to sleep with your eyes open."

So, she could see his point of view, somewhat. But did it tell her what her options were? He was one attractive man, and the word sexy could have been invented just for him, but that didn't mean she was about to go along with his ordained plan for the evening.

Lorelei was honest enough with herself to admit he interested her. Intrigued her. Excited her, even. But "no" still meant "no" and he couldn't cross that line without doing damage to whatever this fragile thing between them was. She wouldn't calmly lay back and let him, either.

What, then? Seduce him before the time he'd appointed in his ultimatum, so at least it was on her terms? Not a very good solution. If only she had more time to explore her feelings and her reaction to him, to be sure that she wanted things to go further.

Disconsolate, she turned over on her stomach and wove her fingers into the thick fur.

Time...she had too much of it, in one sense. Not nearly enough, in another. Where was her famous instinct for knowing exactly whatever she needed to know when she needed it? "About a thousand years away, that's where," she grumbled.

She reviewed her options once more from the top. Do nothing? Bad plan. Use tai chi to fight him off and hope it didn't infuriate him so much that it made things worse? Fight without fighting, by being a limp, cold fish and hoping it turned him off? Well, that was a good possibility. If he felt any kind of emotional tug towards her at all, he wouldn't want it that way.

Or maybe he *could* go that far, trying to prove to himself that he was still in control. She really didn't know how far he could be pushed. He was honorable, by his own code. But she didn't know it well enough to know where he'd draw the line. He meant her no harm, she was certain of that. But that didn't mean he couldn't hurt her out of ignorance or lack of understanding.

If only he still found her repulsive.

Now there was a good possibility. Could she act nutty enough to put him off? At least long enough to buy more time? Maybe. Maybe not. But she didn't have any better ideas.

"I am a crazy woman," Lorelei muttered. "I am out of my mind and dangerous." Then, more confidently, "Run away, Viking! Lunatic alert!"

No, no, no. That was really overdoing it. Lorelei giggled at herself, unable to keep from going over the edge into a Monty Python-type act.

Unfortunately, she mused, she didn't have much of a knack for craziness. Did she? What would be a crazy thing to do, right now, from Erik's standpoint?

Lorelei frowned, creasing her brow in thought. Then she smiled, snapping her fingers. "Got it!" she exclaimed cheerfully. The crazy thing to do, from his perspective, would probably be to ignore everything he'd just said and act as if the whole thing had never happened. He wouldn't know how to take that, would he?

Of course, if she was wrong, she could find herself in some trouble. But then, she already was in trouble. He'd already stated his intention to do his worst.

So what did she really have to lose by being her usual bold self and barging on out there in search of a little entertainment as well as some fresh air? Although she'd have to wear her stage dress again. It would be going too far, she was certain, to defy him while wearing the dress Harold had given her.

She eyed the forbidden garment sadly. What a waste, the most beautiful dress she'd ever had her hands on and she couldn't wear it. And who knew when she'd get another addition to her wardrobe?

Someday she'd find a way to make that barbarian pay. Through the nose, preferably. If only she had him in the twenty-first century, and had his credit card in her possession for an hour...fantasies of vengeful shopping sprees danced in her head.

By the time she'd donned her stretchy stage outfit, minus shoes and pantyhose, and combed through her hair, she wasn't in the mood to talk to Erik again. She looked like the victim of a hit-and-run, and it was all his fault. Disgruntled, she headed back out into the sunlight and towards the other end of the boat.

It actually had a dragon's head, she noticed. A smile broke over her face at the sight. A real dragon's head, with the carved neck curving invitingly over the prow. The sides of the boat had a flat surface wide enough...giving in to impulse, she jumped as lightly as a cat onto the edge and balanced there, letting the wind tangle through her hair and tasting the salt spray.

His heart in his throat, Erik froze at the sight of her, poised against sea and sky. She'd jumped to the dragon's neck, instead of over the side as he'd feared. Now she rode there, balanced precariously and threatened by every wave. He feared to move or call out. If he startled her, she could fall.

Unbelievably, her position seemingly lacked sufficient challenge, for she extended one leg and rode the dragon with one foot. She seemed to float above the water in a strange, slow dance, her liquid movements mimicking the waves. Rising, falling, rolling motions. Unable to look away, afraid to breathe, he watched her.

When the unusual sight drew the others, one by one, he waved at them for silence.

"What is she doing now?" Bjarni muttered in a hushed voice.

"Getting ready to jump," Oleg answered.

Harold smiled. Erik wanted to hit him for the hint of smug, secret knowledge in his face.

Tai chi on a dragon's back. Lorelei wanted to laugh in delight at the opportunity. The boat was unbelievably well made and the dragon's neck was strong enough to support a lot more than her slight weight. It was fun, with just enough of a thread of danger to keep things interesting. She felt like the Karate Kid. Keeping her balance and following correct form with the added element of motion under her feet to contend with gave the exercise heightened awareness.

Finished, she leaped lightly back to the rim. It was about the width of a balance beam and easy to grip with her bare feet. She saw Erik watching her and waved, her annoyance forgotten for the moment. "Hi, Erik!" The water picked up her voice and amplified the sound. She had the whole crew for an audience, it looked like. Good. Maybe he wouldn't want to carry out her intended punishment with all the men watching.

She ran along the side towards him with easy grace and couldn't resist doing a front walk-over for the sheer fun of it. Moving into a handspring, she dropped lightly to the deck in front of him and landed, grinning, in his arms.

He was frowning, she noticed.

"Hey, don't worry," she assured him, "I used to do gymnastics. I was pretty good, too. I was perfectly safe."

"You were not safe. You could have fallen," he informed her in rough tones.

Lorelei sighed. "Listen, life isn't safe."

"That is no reason to court death."

"I wasn't." Indignant, she frowned up at him.

"Then you are too mad to know the difference."

The insanity plea was losing its appeal. "I am not, Erik. I knew what I was doing. I have very good balance and I use catwalks in my concerts all the time." Then she decided a distraction was in order. "Listen, did you know this whole ship is a work of art? Have you seen the carving on the prow? The dragon has individual scales. It's amazing, Erik. I've never seen anything like it. And those loops along the sides, everything is decorated. You Vikings don't do anything halfway, do you?"

She had him confused, if not distracted. Good. Lorelei beamed at him innocently and babbled on.

"Well, I did see something on a National Geographic special once. There was this shipbuilder. He learned how from his father, and his father learned from his grandfather, all the way back for centuries. They didn't use blueprints or anything, they just carved by eye with hand tools. He made boats like this one, only smaller and not so artistic in the trim." She paused, then frowned. "Actually, it was really sad. He didn't have a son to learn from him and he was the last Viking shipbuilder. The last representative of a dying art."

Caught up in the story, she failed to notice the looks that passed among the men. "Anyway, Erik, you don't know how lucky you are to have a ship like this. It really is unbelievable. Is it very old? Do you know who made it?"

"Lorelei." The warning came from Harold and she turned in surprise. "It is forbidden for outsiders to know of our shipbuilding secrets."

She blinked in surprise. "Oh. I shouldn't ask any questions?"

"No." The bearded man was trying not to laugh, she realized. "Tell them it was a story. They think your people captured a shipbuilder. They think you are a spy."

"A spy?" Lorelei stared at him in amazement, then back at Erik's forbidding visage.

"She knows nothing," Harold volunteered on her behalf. "She simply tells stories. Remember, she spoke of making a song for me?"

"That was before she took a dislike to your beard," Erik reminded him.

"She admires my beard. How could she not?" Harold gave Erik a deeply offended look.

"Easily," Lorelei informed him with a smirk. "On the plus side, though, the hair almost muffles the sound of your voice."

Harold shouted with laughter at her irreverent remark.

Everyone else, she couldn't help noticing, was frowning at her.

Maybe the beards meant something to the men. Like a cowboy and his boots. Lorelei gave Erik a weak smile. "Uh, your beard is very nice," she offered, hoping to make up for any unintentional insult.

He didn't look appeased. She tried again. "Ah, it's very impressive, really. Very full and uh, colorful. Streaky." She peered closely at it. "You know, I didn't realize there were so many shades of blond before. White-gold and reddish..." Her voice trailed off as she found herself staring at Erik's beard and remembering how it had felt when he'd kissed her. She'd never kissed a bearded man before. The sensation had been unique.

Unthinkingly, she let her hand follow her eyes and trace the curve of his lips, brushing the soft, wiry hair of his mustache and beard at the same time. Soft, she found herself thinking. So very soft and inviting. With a jolt, she realized she was very nearly drooling on the man publicly.

Lorelei pulled back, blushing and stammering in momentary confusion. "Ah. Uh. Um, okay, I think I'd better go. Back, I mean. Alone. By myself." She started to walk backwards as she spoke, her eyes still fixed on Erik's sensual mouth. Which might have been why she tripped over Bjarni. She recovered swiftly, muttered a quick, "sorry," to the alarmed Viking and continued to retreat.

Fortunately, Erik seemed as confused by their encounter as she was, since he let her go and didn't follow her. It was a relief to escape and collapse safely out of sight, she decided. Well, partly disappointing, too. But a relief, still.

Shivering, she curled on the fur and wondered just what she'd accomplished. If she'd accomplished anything, it was convincing him that she was crazy, all right...about him.

Erik found it an effort to let her go. If he had made any move at all, if he had so much as touched her, he would have been lost to all control and uncaring of any audience. The way she had looked at him, as if she wanted to twine her hands through his beard and devour his mouth, had his whole body taut and aching in response.

When Harold interrupted his thoughts, it was an effort to decipher the meaning in his words.

"You see? She is harmless. No threat to anyone. She knows nothing."

Erik frowned at this earnest defense. She was his, and no concern of anyone else's. Especially she was no concern of Harold's. He decided to make that clear if he had not done so already. "That is for me to decide," he informed Harold, fixing a glacial stare on his brother.

Harold looked disturbed. "There is no need to be hasty."

"I will decide what is needed."

"Of course. Of course." Harold raised his hands. "I well know what a level head you have. Certainly you will think through every possible course of action before deciding which to take."

Erik's gaze narrowed in suspicion. "You will cease to concern yourself. I will deal with the matter."

Bjarni pointed out helpfully, "Who would send a mad spy?"

Harold shot him a glare. Then he gave Erik an innocent look. "True. Nobody would send a poor, pitiful mad woman to spy. And who could have known you would buy her? All the world trades in Hedeby."

They were defending her, Erik realized in disbelief. From him. As if he would threaten her. It was almost amusing. "Enough. We have work to do," he pointed out firmly. The men scattered to do it. Except for Harold, who lingered.

"Erik," he began slowly.

"What now?"

The younger man hesitated. "It is nothing," he said finally. Then he, too, made himself scarce and left Erik alone with his thoughts, which returned again and again to a certain disobedient slave.

Lorelei wasn't too sure what a slave who wanted to get in her master's good graces should do. If she waited for him naked, would it put him in a good mood? Or put her in a worse position? After all, he hadn't said anything about her wearing clothes against orders. Maybe she should just leave well enough alone and hope for the best.

Yes, she decided firmly, remembering the way he'd looked at her, that was definitely best. In fact, maybe she should look for something more to put on, too. A suit of armor would be good. Too bad they didn't seem to have one of those lying around.

With nothing to do but wonder what was coming next, she fidgeted and worried. By the time Erik made his appearance, she was so nervous she had to muffle an involuntary shriek at the sight of him. She also couldn't help shooting to her feet and moving away from the fur that had proven a little too convenient earlier.

He frowned at her and folded his arms in front of his chest. "Come here."

Lorelei gulped. That was an order. But her legs didn't want to move.

"Come here," he repeated. But in a gentler tone. Cautiously, she approached and halted just out of reach. Erik crooked one hand. She let out a long breath and came closer.

"Are you mad?" she inquired.

"You question the soundness of my mind again," he said with resignation. "Cease, and do as I ask. Come here."

Still, she hesitated. "I meant, are you angry." She took another deep breath and then boldly met his eyes. "You can hardly expect me to come within reach if you're angry. You do remember how much bigger you are, don't you?"

Erik smiled. The effect was devastating. It softened his harsh features and for a moment, Lorelei glimpsed a faint echo of a familiar, trusted friend. No, she corrected herself, that wasn't right. Erik didn't resemble either Harold or Dane. They were more like faded, blurred copies of him. Lacking some vital dimension he had. The family resemblance was unbelievably strong, but far from exact. Dane could be Harold's twin, but Erik was distinctly different. Not merely older. Stronger. More ruthless. That was it, the thing that unnerved her so badly. Ruthless, and very compelling, Lorelei admitted. She stepped closer and hoped it was safe.

Slowly, gently, Erik folded her into his arms and tucked her against his chest. "Was that so bad?" he asked.

She shook her head. "No."

He held her until she relaxed. Then he pulled her to the fur and drew her down with him.

Lorelei stiffened again. "Uh, Erik, wait."

His grip tightened and drew her inexorably down. The message was clear. If she went along, the grasp remained firm but gentle. If she resisted, she'd hurt herself. Clever.

"Sit," he said firmly.

She sat.

"Take that off."

She shivered. "Erik, you don't understand. I can't."

He stroked her jaw line gently. "I understand better than you think."

"Do you? I wonder." If he did understand, he'd be one up on her. She didn't understand anything that had happened so far, and some part of her still fervently hoped she'd wake up in a nice, safe hospital somewhere.

She didn't resist when he tugged her dress over her head. At least it was still wearable, she consoled herself. Sort of. His clothes followed, and again she tried to look on the bright side. He wasn't making her help, at least. And this way, they were even. It made her feel slightly less vulnerable and exposed. Especially the way he kept his eyes on hers instead of leering at her body.

"Look at me." Calm and cool, that was her Viking. She found it just as irritating as his tendency to take everything too literally.

"No." No way was she going to look at any more of him than she had already. Just to be safe, Lorelei shut her eyes, too.

He laughed softly, and the sound caressed her brittle nerves. "Look at me."

She shook her head in refusal.

Erik sighed and lifted her into his lap. "Stubborn. Willful. Disobedient." Somehow, he made the words sound like endearments as he cuddled her.

She opened her eyes to glare at him. "Stop confusing me, Erik. First you scare me, then you're nice to me. Stop being nice. Be consistent."

His answering smile was devastating. "You opened your eyes."

To her horror, her lips started to quaver and tears flooded her eyes. Furious, she scrubbed at her cheeks. "Now look what you made me do," she sniffed. "You made me cry again. I never cry. I hate crying."

"Then why do you cry?" The gentle question, accompanied by a soft kiss on the corner of her mouth crumbled the remainder of her composure and she started to cry in earnest.

"B-because you're scaring me," she sobbed.

"Shh. Hush." The low, soothing words made her shudder convulsively.

"Stop it," she whispered, beating against his chest with one fist. "Stop."

"Stop being nice to you?"

"Stop owning me!" The hoarse, tortured cry erupted from the depths of her heart and Lorelei cried harder. "You won't leave me anything. I'll be lost."

Her breath was coming faster, and in some rational corner of her mind Lorelei wondered if she was having a panic attack. Her eyes were tinged with wildness as she pleaded, "Stop it, Erik. Stop it. I can't do it. I can't."

"Hush, now. Hush." He pushed her head against the hollow of his chest and wrapped the silky fur around them both.

"No. I know what you're doing." Lorelei beat at his arms and struggled against his hold.

"What is it that you think I do?"

At the calm, even tone, she closed her eyes and forced herself to match his calm. She was a pebble dropping in a lake. Ripples moving outward, sinking stillness in the center. Still. She held the image and forced her breathing to slow.

When she thought she could speak, she answered through stiff lips, "You're trying to break me, and making me want you to do it. If I let you, you'd be everything to me. Everything." Panic welled up again, and she fought it back. It was so dangerously seductive. He was so strong. She could just let him be strong for both of them. He'd be kind to her. He'd give her anything she needed. He'd be gentle with her when he took her, but they would never be lovers because it would never be a relationship of equals and he would own her, body and soul.

And when he tired of her, it would destroy her. Because he would have taken and taken, and she would have nothing of herself left.

That he would tire of her was as inevitable as the sunrise, Lorelei realized. Because whether he knew it or not, he was like her. He was looking for a strength to match his own. An equal. Erik was a free man, and a free man would never love a slave.

She couldn't tolerate being used and discarded. It wasn't in her. Lorelei breathed deeply again, opened her eyes, and calmly repeated, "No. The answer is no. I told you from the beginning that I wouldn't cooperate."

"That you did." Erik shifted them both so that they lay together in a tangle of limbs. He must have noticed she was cold since he then tucked her more fully into his arms to let his body heat warm her. "I see you like the lynx skin," he remarked as he folded it more closely around her.

"Is that what it is? I didn't know. It's beautiful." Tired, Lorelei curled against him and brushed at the remainder of her tears.

He caught her hands and kissed away the traces of moisture on her cheeks. She went still again, and Erik shook his head in apparent dismay. "Can I not even kiss you without causing you to fear me?"

"Apparently not."

"Then go to sleep."

"This isn't the part where you attack me?" Lorelei asked, trying to be nonchalant but failing miserably.

"Attack was never my plan." Erik smiled at her and held her chin to keep her from looking away. "Taking you, willing or otherwise, was not my plan this night."

She raised a skeptical brow. "Really? You could have fooled me."

"Really." He tossed the word back to her, mockingly. "You will become used to me and to your duties. It is your duty to share my bed, so you will grow accustomed to sharing it, beginning now."

Lorelei's brows shot up as she took that piece of information in. "Become used to you. Uh huh."

"Good. You are following me."

"I am not following much of anything."

"Then sleep." Erik delivered the calm suggestion as he settled her in the curve of his arm again, pillowing her head on his chest.

Sleep, she thought in disbelief. Sure. Right. Just go to sleep and ignore the naked man with the big sword who thinks he owns you. "I can't sleep."

Her disgruntled voice made him smile. "Then perhaps I should introduce you to your other duties."

"That isn't funny," she informed him in a small voice.

"You have odd ideas about when to jest," he returned. He let one hand glide along her waist, then stroke lower to cup the curve of her hip. When he moved to continue downward, she grabbed at his wrist with both of her hands.

"Wait. I'm getting tired. Really, really sleepy. I think I can go right to sleep, in fact," she babbled.

With an effort, Erik refrained from laughing out loud. "Ah. Then your other duties can wait."

"You're too kind," she sneered. Then she quickly settled down and feigned a sleeper's slow, deep breathing.

He listened to the sound until he knew she truly slept. The simple pleasure he took in having this slight, troublesome woman in his arms warmed him. He felt a deep contentment in spite of the unsatisfied desire she stirred in him. He had what he had wanted, after all. An amusing companion. Bedding her would prove as entertaining as he had hoped. She never behaved as he expected but he could not imagine tiring of her, that much was certain. She argued, fought and challenged him every step of the way. It made every battle won all the more satisfying and would make her ultimate conquest all the sweeter.

At the memory of her sudden urge to sleep, he laughed softly.

Harold would have been shocked.

Not at his decision that there was no rush to take what was already his, but that he was showing definite signs of having fun.

Chapter Seven

Waking up, Lorelei stretched and felt a distinct urge to purr. She lay wrapped in luxurious comfort. The silky fur caressed her on one side and velvety heat rubbed against her on the other. Erik. With the memory came faint surprise that she'd gone right to sleep after all, and now it seemed like the most natural thing in the world to wake up curled around the barbarian.

Well, when in Rome...with a mental shrug, she gave in to her urges and emitted a low, happy purr as she snuggled closer.

"Now you decide you wish to warm my bed," Erik rumbled. His arms tightened around her and Lorelei decided that those muscles were definitely a turn-on. Kind of in the same way the sun was definitely a light source.

"So far, so good," she returned cheerfully.

"Then you will adjust to your place and learn to enjoy your duties."

Lorelei groaned. "Good up until now. Erik, tell me, is it just you, or are all Vikings smug, self-satisfied macho men?"

Without warning, she found herself on her back with an annoyed macho man looming over her. "If I found satisfaction with myself, I would have no need of you," he informed her ominously. "Do you wish me to prove what I need from you?"

Desire and fear rose in equal parts in response. His penis was hard and hot against her bare skin, all male and blatant need. But along with the proof of his desire came a reminder that he saw her as just another way to find relief, and that cooled her off in a hurry.

"Um, I think you just did," she answered with a wry smile. "And anyway, that wasn't a slam on your masculinity. It was a comment on your lamentable attitude. I just wondered if it was a cultural thing."

At his frown, she tried to explain further, "I mean, I don't know how you men are. With women."

A slow, devastatingly sexy smile replaced the frown and threatened her equilibrium. "I will show you how we are with women."

Lorelei gulped. "No, that's okay. I'm sure you know what you're doing."

To her horror, he slid one muscled thigh between hers and forced them apart, moving to rest heavily against the cradle of her hips. The sensation of being covered from head to toe with muscular, masculine Viking while her spread legs brought him into intimate contact made it difficult to remember why this was a bad idea. But she was hazily sure that it was. "No, wait."

"I tire of waiting," he informed her huskily. His broad chest brushed lightly against her breasts and teased her nipples as he shifted to probe her labia with the broad, hard head of his cock. The length of him slid along her nether lips in a seductive tease of a caress.

This was good. No, this was bad. Wasn't it? Lorelei closed her eyes. "This isn't happening. It isn't real. None of this is real. I've been on a psychedelic trip this whole time, and—" she ran out of steam, and finished desperately, "Erik, please, please don't."

"You will soon beg me to continue," he saidwith a knowing smile.

That annoyed her enough to glare at him. "Oh, I will, huh? Let me tell you something, Casanova. In case you didn't notice, you're a whole lot readier than I am for this encounter. It doesn't look like anyone but you is going to have any fun here."

He sighed in regret. "You make me wish I had time to prove the truth of my words. But you wrong me to think I would give no thought to your pleasure."

He had her full attention. Lorelei frowned at him. "What do you mean?"

He gave her a typically serious, literal answer. "Think you that I know not how slaves are treated?" While he let her mull that one over, Erik sat up and pulled her into his lap, stroking her as if she were a cat. "I gave you my word that you were not for the use of my men. I would not allow that slaver to take you. Think you I will not have a care for you?"

"Erik?" She tipped her face up to meet his eyes searchingly. "What exactly do you mean, you wouldn't let him take me. Take me where?"

"On the ground. Before an audience." His face hardened along with his voice.

"On...on the..." She stopped, took a breath, and let it out in a rush. "Oh, Lord in heaven. Erik, are you saying what I think you're saying? He was actually going to...I mean...right there?" A shudder shook her at the thought. It was too awful to contemplate. The idea of rape was bad enough, but in public, as some kind of performance? Sickeningly worse.

"I have seen it done before," Erik answered evenly.

For once, she was struck dumb. Lorelei buried her face in the curve of his neck and clung to him while she tried to get a grip on her rocketing imagination.

"Erik. You really didn't have to tell me that." Shakily, Lorelei loosened her stranglehold on him and lifted her head enough to give him a reproachful look. "The curse of the creative. I have this vivid imagination. Now I'm going to see that every time I close my eyes." She shuddered again and gave him a grateful hug. "Did I thank you? If I didn't, Erik, a thousand thanks. Thank you, thank you, thank you."

Then she straightened abruptly and added, "But this doesn't change anything. I still don't want to be a slave. I appreciate your help, really. But if you could just drop me off anywhere convenient, I'll be on my way."

She wasn't prepared for him to laugh at her.

"Ah, Lorelei." She was so taken by the deep, rich sound of his laughter that she almost didn't realize he'd used her name for the first time. "You please me."

Her eyes narrowed in ire. "Oh, I do, do I? Great. Just great. I can't tell you how happy that makes me."

"It makes me happy, as well." The satisfaction in his voice grated on her. It really did. "Now you will tell me why you wish not to be owned by me."

She sighed. "Oh, let me count the ways. For starters, Erik, you can't own a person."

"I can. I do."

"This is going to be difficult, I can see that right now. You don't own me."

"I do. I bought you. Even had I not, I won you by force. By every law, you belong to me now."

She rolled her eyes. "Oh, and I can't argue with the law, can I?"

"No," her earnest, literal Viking was happy to inform her. "Even were you not a slave and therefore without rights, the Rule of Law is held once a year. You would have to make your protest then."

"Rule of Law. What about the Bill of Rights?" She glared at him and went on, "All men are created equal and endowed with certain rights. And those rights include life, liberty and the pursuit of happiness. It's the American way. We're all equal, and we're all free."

"We also are all equal and free," Erik said. "But you are not a Dane, and you are my slave."

She closed her eyes and smacked her forehead with one palm. "How did I miss that little fact?"

"I find it strange myself. You belong to me, and the sooner you accept that, the sooner you will come to enjoy it."

Lorelei leaned back and eyed him seriously. "Erik, do you really believe I'll just accept it?"

He smiled broadly. "No." He caressed her cheek with one open hand. "I look forward to persuading you." The kiss that followed was pure persuasion. Soft and full of subtle seduction, his lips teased hers until they parted and clung to his. With a low sound of encouragement, he cupped the back of her head with one hand and held her for his ravishment. His tongue tasted and withdrew, returned and twined with hers in a deep, wild mating that gradually awakened and fed an answering hunger.

She shivered and moaned softly, the sound lost in his kiss, as he cupped and gently squeezed one bare breast. His rough palm teased her nipple into tautness for his thumb to rub, back and forth, until she was quivering from the sensation.

When he lifted his head, she opened dazed eyes to meet his.

"Wow," she whispered, shaken.

He nodded. "For once, I think I understand your meaning." They fell silent and he hugged her close, turning her so that she sat with her back against his chest. When he took advantage of the position to stroke his hands over her breasts, she couldn't find it in herself to protest. The touch felt too good. Too comfortingly warm and human. Too sensually stirring. His hands on her body felt oddly right in a way that no other man's ever had. The wrongness had always jarred her and brought things to a halt before they really even got started. For once, she was responding to a man like a red-blooded woman, and the relief that she wasn't frigid after all kept her from arguing even when he slid one hand between her legs and cupped her where no man had gone before.

The Star Trek analogy made her smile. Then his thumb rubbing across the sensitive nub of her clitoris the same way he'd manipulated her nipple made her gasp.

He chuckled, a deep, satisfied sound that vibrated against her back. "I find persuading you most enjoyable. I hope you require much more persuasion."

She made a noncommittal sound. The twin sensations of one hand toying with her breasts, teasing her into a state of ever more heightened sensitivity, coupled with his hand between her thighs working her until she grew slick and wet with arousal were enough to drive her out of her mind.

Back and forth his fingers slid, teasing her with her own wetness, circling her sensitized clit, thrusting downward to part her labia and slip just barely inside and then withdrawing again. Her breath came more and more quickly and she let out a moan of pleasure.

"Now you are as ready as I am," he muttered thickly. She didn't argue. Erik shifted and drew her down, placed her on her back, then spread her thighs wide and settled himself over her. His hard shaft probed at her entry, now swollen and slick in readiness for his invading cock.

Our mission, to explore strange new worlds, Lorelei thought. Then he drove into her with one powerful thrust and she immediately found the Star Trek manifesto terribly inadequate.

"Erik," she gasped, her eyes going wide with shock, "I think you just killed me."

"No, you are killing me," he gritted out. "You are too tight."

"I'm too tight? You're too big. You're going to split me in half."

He growled and thrust deeper and she gasped. "Stop that. I'm dying."

"If you were dying, you would be silent," he pointed out. She saw a fine sheen of sweat on his brow as he struggled for control. "It has been too long for me. I would say it has also been too long for you."

"This is no time to argue." Lorelei moaned.

"For once, we are agreed." To her relief, he withdrew. The relief was short-lived, however. He surged forward again, breaking through the barrier she wasn't even sure was there as he filled her completely. She closed her eyes and braced herself, but he remained still.

After a moment, she realized it didn't hurt, exactly. In fact, as she relaxed, it felt wonderful. She smiled and arched under his weight in an instinctive movement, seeking more contact, more depth, more...something. "Erik," she whispered. She opened her eyes to see him frowning down at her. "Now what?"

"How can you be virgin?" the barbarian wanted to know. He didn't look happy, either, now that she thought about it.

"By not doing this before," she answered, stating the obvious. "Can we please discuss it later? I think I like it. Why don't we keep going, and I'll let you know afterwards." As she made the suggestion, she moved sinuously underneath him and hugged his hips with her thighs.

"You cannot be a virgin," he muttered, still looking unhappy.

"Technically, I don't think I qualify now, so don't let that stop you," Lorelei suggested helpfully.

"A virgin wanton." He looked confounded.

"Ex-virgin wanton. Thanks to you. Erik, please, I want more."

He groaned and sank deeper. If she'd thought he was already buried in her to the hilt, she was wrong. She could feel him all the way to the entrance of her womb.

"Wow," she repeated softly.

"Indeed." Erik's mouth closed over hers again, and then he was driving into her with all the pent-up fury of a storm at sea. An answering storm rose inside of her, years of need and denial buried and waiting for this moment, this man. The storm built with each thrust, two beings striving to give and take and become one in increasing urgency. Lorelei found herself gasping with effort as she strained for something nearly attainable. Almost, almost...then the storm broke over her in wave after wave of pleasure that swept her out into depths she'd never imagined. Until, at last, she came to rest intimately joined with the man who had claimed her in some primal, primitive way.

Incredible. So this was what she'd been missing. All this time, she'd seen only the tip of the iceberg called desire, and who knew what other discoveries lay hidden? Suddenly, Lorelei saw a whole new dimension in her music that she hadn't fully understood at the time she'd written it. She'd just followed the pattern it demanded without really knowing why, trusting her instincts to know that when it felt right, it was, whether it made sense or not.

No wonder she'd been so restless, so discontented. She had known on some level that she hadn't been complete. She'd needed this. Passion. A true connection with a man. The man. Her man.

Just as she'd known on that same instinctual level that now was the right time. That Erik was the right man, whether it made sense or not. And by any logical view, it didn't.

Lost in thought and flooded with lethargy, the last thing Lorelei expected was to find herself suddenly bereft of the communion she'd so recently discovered with Erik as he levered himself away to place his hand at her throat and his sword-point at her heart.

"Who are you?" he demanded, his voice fierce and taut with determination.

She blinked in puzzlement. "Who am I? Who are you? What happened to the man I just made love with?"

The hand gripping her throat flexed and subtly decreased her air supply. "Answer the question." The menace in that near-whisper chilled her as effectively as the cold metal on her bare skin.

Wrong, she thought, this is all wrong. A moment before, she would have sworn she knew this man and that he would never knowingly hurt her. Now death was in his touch and in the coldness of his gaze. It gave a sense of warped unreality to the scene, as if it were something happening to someone else.

"Erik," she said quietly, closing her eyes against the sight, "I don't understand the question. I told you my name already."

The sharpened point pressed downward slightly. Her eyes flew wide in shock, and when she looked down, she saw a drop of blood forming against the tip. He wasn't hurting her. But the threat was clear. "What are you doing?"

His hand tightened further, cutting off her voice. "You will speak only to answer. Nod if you understand."

She nodded. The grip loosened, and she sucked in air gratefully.

"Who are you?"

Maybe it was the thought that he could threaten to hurt her. Maybe it was the way he could go from lover to executioner in a moment. Maybe it was just plain wounded ego that what had been an epic event in her life obviously meant nothing to him. But Lorelei was suddenly blazingly angry. Her eyes fairly shot sparks and she was so furious that it made her tremble.

"Someone who doesn't want to play," she snarled. She wasn't going to say another word, either. She'd wear polyester and spend the rest of her life as an Elvis impersonator before she'd tell him anything.

"You will answer the question."

"No."

Erik realized her defiance should not have come as a surprise. When did she ever comply? It was one reason he could not trust her sudden surrender in his arms. There was also the fact that she knew more of shipbuilding than she should. The fact that she knew their language, although she did speak it badly and with a strange accent. The fact that she held a fatal fascination for a man that drove him to forget his duties and could, in time, make him forsake all honor.

She was no simple slave and he could not believe her presence in Hedeby, coinciding with his own, to be mere chance. Neither did he think her mad. Nay, she had cunning beyond anything he had suspected, and she represented an unknown enemy. He would find out the truth of the matter.

"You will tell me who you are, and who you spy for," Erik stated softly.

That surprised her. "Spy? Like James Bond?"

"Now we progress. Tell me of this James Bond."

"What? Well, he's English. Her Majesty's secret service, you know?"

"English." He frowned at the term.

"Oh. What you call Saxons, maybe?"

The absurdity of the conversation struck her, and suddenly it was hard not to laugh. A spy. He thought she was some kind of Mata Hari. Well, she'd feed him a load of misinformation, and it was exactly what he deserved. As quickly as it had ebbed, her wrath returned. He'd ruined a beautiful experience. No, worse, he'd made it into something ugly and made her wish it had never happened. She could hate him for that.

Pure vindictiveness led her to continue. "Yes, Saxons. They have a ring of secret agents who infiltrate every country in the world and report back information about weapons, armies and who has what and how much of it, and where." If nothing else, she'd do her best to make him paranoid, she decided. She went on, "Every agent is known by a number as a protection against having their identity uncovered."

"And who is this James Bond?"

She smiled. "My lover." In her dreams, she added silently.

"You lie."

Oh. Right. He knew better. "James and I have an understanding."

"If he comes for you, I will kill him," he informed her harshly. "And you will watch."

Lorelei gave him a poisonous smile. "Better men than you have tried."

He scowled, breaking the emotionless mask of indifference. "So you still prefer your Saxon who had not the wit nor the desire to make you his. He must be a boy and not a man. Or a eunuch and no man at all."

She scowled back. "Make me his? How primitive."

"Primitive, yes." With a lightning movement, Erik flipped his sword to the side and jerked her beneath him. "Basic. Elemental. You will forget this man and you will forget this foolish loyalty to him. I did what he failed to do. I made you mine. You belong to me."

She was suddenly tired of fighting. Tired of the internal war of anger and hurt. It colored her smoky voice with a finality. "You didn't make me yours. You made me nothing."

His eyes narrowed, piercing her with their intensity. "You will admit you belong to me."

She feigned a yawn. "Will I?" She let her lashes drift down to shield her eyes in apparent indifference, but in reality out of sheer stubbornness and pride. She didn't want him to see her hurt. She wouldn't give him the satisfaction. Trying for another dig, she added, "Are you going to 'make me yours' again? Wake me up when you're finished. Although it's likely to be over before I really get to sleep."

For a minute, she thought he just might. Then he stood and growled, "Freya, you are colder than the north sea. No wonder your lover sent you to spy for him. Perhaps he hoped to freeze us all in our beds. Or it may be that he hoped enough men would make you grateful for his limited attentions."

She heard him dress in short, sharp movements, heard the ring of steel as he retrieved his sword, and finally, the welcome sound of the door closing behind him.

Alone, she lay still for a moment. Then an almost compulsive need to wash his touch away coupled with a frenzied desire to escape the scene of her humiliation drove her to her feet.

She threw on her only clothing once more, making a face of distaste at the state her dress was in. Well, the sea would take care of it, and of her, too. In another minute, she was out the door and balanced on the ship's ledge. Then she was diving cleanly into the water below.

Cold. The water really was cold. As cold as Erik had accused her of being. She grimaced, thinking of Erik's parting shot. Nice to know her worst fears were true, after all. The one man she slept with compared the experience to flirting with hypothermia.

And this was really stupid. She surfaced and gasped with the shock of the cold that was going all the way through to her bones. Big mistake. The next time she got mad at Mr. Lord and Master Viking, she was throwing *him* overboard instead.

She heard the shouts immediately, once she came up and started to tread water. They were impossible to miss, actually, since they were directly overhead and amplified by the presence of water.

"Keep looking! How can you miss a woman in the middle of the sea?"

"I tell you, I can see nothing." That was Barney, she thought. Sounding aggrieved.

"You will keep looking until she is found," another voice roared. "You let her go overboard."

Erik's voice. And he sounded furious.

"She will be drowned by now," another man pointed out.

"Then you will help find the body." Erik again, in an icy rage. "We stay here until we find her."

"You are the one who made her jump." That sounded like Harold, Lorelei thought. "The finest skald I have ever heard, and what do you do? Abuse her until she flings herself into the sea. I should never have left her to you."

It was entertaining to listen to them, but she was far too cold. Lorelei rose up in the water as high as she could and shouted, "Harold! Toss me a rope, and I'll sing for you again!"

There was a moment of silence. Then a row of heads appeared, outlined by the sun. "Lorelei?"

"Were you expecting the Avon lady? It's cold in here. Toss me a rope, please." She smiled back at her audience, squinting against the sun that blinded her to individual faces.

The rope splashed just in front of her a second later. "Thanks!" She latched onto it and clung, shivering, as she let herself be hauled up. "That water is really c-c-cold," she chattered, as she went. "I'm frozen."

A now-familiar hand closed over hers as it neared the top and pulled her the rest of the way.

"If you were frozen," Erik informed her ominously, "You would make less noise."

Chapter Eight

He wasn't in a good mood, Lorelei decided. Erik dragged her back to the cabin, pausing only to yank his shirt off and haul it over her head, whether to keep her from freezing or to keep anyone from ogling the curves sharply outlined by the wet fabric of her dress, she couldn't say.

Once they were alone, or as alone as they could be on a crowded boat, he stripped it off her again. Her dress followed, cut down the center by his ornamental dagger.

"Great," Lorelei muttered through blue lips. "You're hard on my wardrobe, do you know that?"

"Be silent." His voice was nearly a deafening shout.

Lorelei blinked. "Sheesh. Somebody got up on the wrong side of the bed." She rubbed at the gooseflesh puckering her arms and shivered.

"Stand still." Erik retrieved his shirt and rubbed her down with the rough fabric. The brisk motion dried and warmed her simultaneously, but she was still cold.

Erik finished drying her, then pulled her down to the lynx skin she preferred to sleep on. Her hair would take time to dry. Meanwhile, she needed warmth. He wrapped her in his embrace, trapping her legs between his own. He drew another fur up to cover them and spread her hair over it, lifting it away from her bare skin. A shudder racked her slight frame and he frowned in concern. Worry made his voice harsh as he demanded, "Do you wish to die?"

"Do you wish to make me deaf? Stop yelling, Erik."

He closed his eyes in relief. Her tongue remained as sharp as ever. She was safe and unhurt. He hugged her closer, absorbing her tremors and letting her draw heat from his body. "I do not yell."

"Oh. Right. That was my imagination running away with me." Lorelei grinned at that, then shivered again in earnest. "Erik, I'm cold." She paused as she realized what she'd said. Her worst fears realized, she'd finally slept with a man and he thought she was frigid. Before she could stop them, tears were welling up and flooding her eyes. She struggled for control for a minute. Then she asked herself why it mattered. Since she couldn't think of a good reason, she let loose and bawled.

Erik felt the tears falling on his chest before he heard her sobbing. "Lorelei? Hush. Hush, woman. I have you now. You are safe, sweet."

A low, choking sob answered his words of comfort. The sound tore at his innards and made him long for an enemy he could face and defeat with fists and swords. Her James Bond would do. He could slaughter the man for his callous use of her. Then would she forget him.

"Hush, do not cry." His tender whisper caressed the shell of her ear. "Hush, sweet. You are mine, and I will never let you go."

She sobbed again, a low, broken sound.

"Shh," he murmured. He stroked her from hip to ribs in a long, gentle motion intended to soothe. Instead, he found himself inflamed by the feel of her. He turned her to fit his palms over the fullness of her breasts. Her nipples budded under his hands and he groaned at her response. All thought of comfort fled. He would make her forget all others. He would make her his, again and again, until she welcomed his possession.

Hunger rose in him, sharp and urgent. He tore at his breeches, positioned her over himself and thrust upwards into her. She struggled briefly. His hands held her hips still as he withdrew and then returned to sheathe himself fully. She parted for him, closed around him and encased him in sweet, tight heat.

With an effort, he waited for her to adjust as he held her. Dimly, he realized that her tears were still falling and she was crying softly.

"Ah, woman," he whispered. His hands gentled, cradling her. "You make me lose control. You make me as thoughtless and greedy as an untried youth. Am I hurting you?"

She sniffled and shook her head slightly.

Erik smiled and kissed her, giving her the tenderness he should have thought to offer sooner. "I will be gentle," he promised softly. "You make me forget that you have never known a man before. There will be no more pain, sweet."

Lorelei raised her face to his, hurt glistening in her eyes. "You're hurting me now."

Carefully, he withdrew and turned on his side to hold her, cuddling her full-length. "Better?"

She shook her head. "That isn't where it hurts. Well, only indirectly."

He frowned again. "You will explain."

She sighed. "Why is it that everything with you sounds like an order?" She reached up to tangle her fingers in his full beard.

"Because it is an order. Explain."

She sighed again and rested her cheek against the smooth, muscled wall of his chest. "All right, you hurt my feelings, you overgrown barbarian."

"Feelings." Erik repeated the word blankly. "How did I do this hurting your feelings?"

"Good question," she muttered. "I'm a tough nut to crack. But since I met you, all I do is—never mind. Let's just say I'm a tad emotional, and leave it at that. Maybe it's PMS. Maybe time-travel causes mood swings. I don't know. But for once in my life, I wanted to make love. I felt real desire for an actual man, and it was wonderful."

Erik smiled against the midnight silk of her hair. Wonderful sounded like a good word for it. Then her next words deflated him completely.

"It was wonderful, and then you ruined it."

She may have misspoken, he reminded himself. Used the wrong word unthinkingly. She did speak Norse badly. "Ruined?"

She nodded and sighed again. "Ruined. From paradise to purgatory in the blink of an eye. One minute, we're as united as two people can get, and the next, you have your hand on my throat and your sword pointed at me. Thank you, but I don't care to repeat the experience. If I was that bad in bed, you can just drop me off at the nearest port and go find yourself another love slave."

"That bad?"

Lorelei levered herself up on one elbow to glare at him. "Do you want me to say it? All right. You said I was a secret weapon sent to turn every Viking dumb enough to come near me into ice."

"I said no such thing."

"Yes, you did. You said I was frigid." At the memory, another tear slid down her cheek.

Erik reached out to brush it away with one finger. Then he curled his hand beneath her chin to lift it for his kiss. Gently, his lips brushed hers in the barest of caresses. "Cold?"

"No, I'm warmer now." Then she blinked in comprehension. "Oh, right. Frigid. Cold. Well, you were right, I am, so just leave me alone."

"And how am I to do that?" Erik brought her full against himself again, rubbing his throbbing arousal against her belly. "I want you. You are mine."

"So you're going to use me for sex, and then criticize my performance? I don't think so."

"I do not think so, either," Erik agreed fervently. "Your performance is not lacking. Well, at this moment, it is. You should be lusting for me. Do you not feel a bit of lust?" His hands explored the swollen peaks of her breasts.

"No. I don't feel any lust anymore. I feel hurt." Lorelei rolled away, turning her back to him as she burrowed into the furs.

Her Viking didn't take the hint, however. He pulled her back and held her securely in his arms, his strong thighs curled under hers, his chest to her back. "You are not cold," he informed her.

Lorelei gritted her teeth. "Sure, you say that now. But you were singing a different tune the last time we were under these blankets."

Erik rubbed her stomach in absent, concentric circles. "I sang no tunes."

"There you go again, being literal. No, you didn't sing. You just threatened to kill me."

He sighed at that reminder. "I did not threaten. I promised. If your lover comes to claim you, I will kill him. But you, I did not speak of killing."

"No, you just used extremely effective body language."

He pushed her onto her back and leaned over her. "I questioned you. That was my duty. And you admitted to being placed here by a spy."

She narrowed her eyes in irritation. "I would have admitted to being an Oscar Meyer wiener, too, for the record. You had a very large, sharp sword ready to carve my heart out."

Erik frowned at her words. "You will explain this Oscar Meyer wiener."

"'Oh, I wish I were an Oscar Meyer wiener,'" she sang readily. At his blank look, she added, "It's a jingle. A product endorsement. An advertisement of wares for sale. An Oscar Meyer wiener is a food product. I would have admitted to being anything, in other words. I like living."

He thought that one over. "Do you tell me you lied? There is no Saxon spy?"

"There's no spy, but that isn't the point. You obviously feel very differently about things than I do. You could make passionate love with me one minute and turn into a stranger capable of killing me the next. I don't understand that, Erik, and frankly I don't want to." Lorelei attempted to pull away again.

He didn't let her. The same muscles that made her salivate made an effective weapon against her. His arms caught and trapped her and kept her close.

She struggled in vain. Finally, she frowned at him. Glared, actually. "Let go."

"No. You feel hurt by me. Therefore, you need my comfort." Erik cuddled her in spite of the fact that she remained stiff, resistant and silent. As time went on and she didn't relent, Erik tried again. "I regret your hurt. It was not my intent. I had a duty to question you."

That stirred her curiosity. Lorelei sat up and looked at him in silent invitation to continue.

He was unused to making explanations for his actions. And to explain to a woman, a slave, at that, seemed absurd. Yet, he wished to soothe her. "Too many things made no sense. You knew things you should not, and know not the things you should. It matters not to me if you were sent by a spy. I would keep you, regardless. But I would make certain you caused no trouble, and I would deal with the man who failed to protect you."

Lorelei quirked a brow at him. "The man who failed to protect me?"

He nodded. "If a man sent you into danger he feared to face himself, leaving you without protection, he deserves to die. But you say there is no Saxon spy, so I will not have to make you watch me kill him."

A slow, mischievous smile turned up the corners of her mouth. "Well, in a manner of speaking, there is a James Bond."

He reached for his sword reflexively.

"No, no, not like you think," Lorelei rushed out. "It's a story. Kind of like, oh, maybe Thor and Loki. Loki makes trouble, and Thor goes around being the hero, right? Well, James Bond is a hero."

Erik reached for her and drew her back down to lay with him. "This James Bond is a hero in Saxon stories?"

She nodded. "A very popular one."

"He is a god?"

"Only in Hollywood."

They fell silent for a short time.

"Then, it is true, what Harold said," Erik stated.

She looked up at him, silent inquiry in her eyes.

"He called you a skald."

She sprawled across his chest in a relaxed heap again. "That's the word he used. By the way, did he throw the rope, or did you? If he did, I owe him a song."

"I did. You owe me a song."

"Mm." She made a noncommittal noise and nestled her cheek into the hollow of his shoulder. It felt so good to be warm again. To have a truce with Erik. To be clean from her swim. She could go back to sleep so easily...

His next order cut through her daydream and dumped her without warning back into reality. "Now you will explain how you came to be in the water and nearly drowned."

So much for a pleasant catnap. She sighed inwardly. "I wasn't in any danger of drowning. I'm an excellent swimmer, and I'm used to the ocean."

He gripped her shoulders painfully. "Do you tell me that you jumped purposely?" Erik demanded.

"Ow. Lighten up, will you?" Lorelei twisted from side to side, but the pressure didn't lesson. Instead, it increased. "Okay, I get the point. Let go."

"I doubt you get the point," he grumbled. "But you will explain." He did loosen his hold, however.

"I'm explaining. I had a sudden urge to go swimming."

He went still. "You had a sudden urge to go swimming," he repeated.

"Yes."

"And when did this sudden urge come upon you?" he asked in a voice like a steel whip.

"Oh, let me see." Lorelei rolled away to give him her back again. "It must have been about the same time that the sudden urge to scare the life out of me came over you."

"You jumped because I questioned you?"

"I didn't jump, I went swimming. I wanted to get clean. It gave me the creeps, Erik." She turned back and met his eyes squarely. "You really don't understand. You touched me. You were *inside* me. Then you put a sword to me and drew blood. I realize this is all probably just another day in the life of your average Viking, but it gave me the creeping horrors."

Erik studied her face silently, his own expressionless. "You felt the need to wash away my touch."

She nodded. "That says it pretty well."

"And now do you feel the need to swim again?"

He wanted to know if it bothered her that badly for him to touch her, she realized. It was tempting to lie. It might make him keep his distance. But she had a sneaking suspicion that under that emotionless mask lurked a vulnerable Viking.

"No," Lorelei admitted. "I don't mind you touching me. I just can't take the sudden change of heart, Erik. I'm not built like that. I can't do it. If you're going to turn on me again, then just stay away from me."

Erik traced the hollow beneath her cheekbone with one gentle finger. "This is why you wished not to belong to me? You feared to give yourself to a stranger, and then be cast off?"

"You make it sound like used clothing. But that's the general idea, I guess," she agreed. "There's also the little matter of ownership. It kind of makes for an unequal relationship." She paused, and turned troubled eyes to his. "I'll be honest with you. I like you. Even when you're a little authoritarian. But I'm never going to be compliant and content with slavery."

Erik studied her face briefly. "You think you cannot be content," he replied calmly. "You will learn. You will adjust."

"Yeah, yeah, yeah. In your dreams, I might add," Lorelei mumbled. But she didn't complain when he started to pick up where he'd left off, before he found out he wasn't hurting her. The problem was, he presented her with temptation on a scale she couldn't even measure. There was a seductive lure in the idea of belonging to him. In the idea of abdicating responsibility for once. To not have to be the one in charge, to relax and just go along with his desires and let him fulfill hers in the process. Desires she hadn't even suspected she had.

Just for a little while, what could it hurt to pretend? Couldn't she enjoy what he offered, just for now? The rest, she could sort out later, Lorelei decided.

And for all she knew, she could find herself back in the future at any moment. That thought made her shiver. In spite of everything, she had found something fragile and precious here. Something that could be lost forever in the blink of an eye. Since she had no idea how she'd gotten there, it was entirely possible she could find herself back where she'd started without warning. She might not have another chance to taste her Viking's kisses.

The possibility that any moment with him might be the last made her part her lips under Erik's and invite his swirling, thrusting tongue to take more, to know all of her. The same urgency communicated itself in the fierce pressure of her hands gripping his shoulders, the tilt of her hips encouraging his sensual invasion.

When he settled himself between her legs again, he took his time entering her. The care he took with her moved her deeply. He was no crude, uncaring captor, but a sensitive and sensual lover, protective and possessive at the same time. He cherished her with sweet kisses while he held her hips in a bruising grip and drove himself deeper with every thrust. He dominated and demanded. He coaxed and seduced. He took her to the edge of reason and beyond, to a world of sensation and emotion where he led and she followed blindly.

He taught her pleasure. And in his burning embrace, she was his willing slave, surrendering gladly to his strength. He took, and she gave. He gave, and she took. His pleasure became her own and when he found his fulfillment, the deep pulsing triggered hers.

Afterwards, he turned her gently to rest against his side. His lips feathered kisses along her smooth brow as his hands touched, held and caressed. This time, he gave her the closeness and comfort that paid homage to the splendor that came before. Secure and satiated, Lorelei curled into his hold and enjoyed the sweet sensation of being closely held after being thoroughly loved.

When he wove his fingers through her hair and tugged her face up for a kiss, she sighed blissfully. He had wonderful lips, she decided. Firm, smooth, and warm. They made her tingle and left trails of fire behind when he lifted his head again to smile at her.

Before he could speak, she put her fingers over his mouth. "Don't say anything," she warned him. "This is a perfect moment. That was beautiful, and don't you dare say something horrible to make it ugly again."

Then she snuggled against his side contentedly.

He hauled her back up. She groaned. He had that look in his eyes again. She was getting to know it. An interrogation was coming.

"You will not feel ashamed to share my bed," he informed her firmly.

"Well, of course not," she agreed . "Why would I?"

Her answer seemed to confuse him. He frowned at her. "I will not have you leaping into the ocean. You will not feel sullied and ugly."

She decided to humor him. Lorelei patted his chest soothingly. "Okay."

The frown deepened. Funny, now that she was getting to know him, it wasn't nearly as intimidating. It was sort of cute, actually, the way he knit his brows and focused those burning blue eyes on her. Well, maybe cute wasn't the right word. Compelling said it better. It was sort of stimulating to be the focus of that intense look.

"Ugliness does not belong between us," Erik went on. He was winding up for a full lecture. Lorelei sighed inwardly, but did her best to look wide-eyed and attentive. And at least, for once, he was saying something she could agree with.

"I find you beautiful. You please me, and I please you as well." Now that was arrogant. But truthful. She couldn't deny that he did please her, especially when she'd been moaning underneath him minutes before.

"Yes, Erik," she agreed meekly, while trying not to laugh.

"It is your duty to give yourself to me. It pleases me that you find pleasure in your duty. You will learn to become content," he assured her.

Well, it had been good while it lasted. Reality could only be postponed for so long before intruding on her fleeting fantasy.

"You will also learn to obey."

Lorelei groaned again. "Oh, Erik. Can't you just leave it alone for an hour? Why do you keep harping on this obey business?"

"I have no harp. You will cease these foolish jests," he instructed her. "You will obey me, Lorelei. I will allow you some freedom. I will not mistreat you. But I will be obeyed."

"Kicked out of paradise again," she mumbled. She sat up and reached for his shirt, since she didn't have any more clothes of her own.

His hands caught hers and stilled them. She turned inquiring eyes to him. "Now what?"

"Now you will ask my permission to dress."

Her gaze narrowed into irritation. "Don't you think that's going a little too far?"

He shook his head. "Not for you." Then he lifted her onto his lap again and gripped her chin to keep her from evading his earnest look. "Lorelei, it is different at home. You are subject to the laws. You cannot act without thinking. You cannot behave as if you are free. For your own safety, you will obey me."

He really meant it. Lorelei studied him for a moment. Grudgingly, she had to admit that he was the expert on his culture, not her. Maybe there were reasons for his annoying insistence on obedience. He'd mentioned laws. Could flaunting him actually make her a criminal?

And if so, what would the punishment for a disobedient slave be? Somehow she had the uneasy feeling it wouldn't be ten hours of community service and group therapy.

"Erik, I'll try," she promised. "That's the best I can do. I haven't obeyed anybody in longer than I can remember, but I'll try."

"This I can believe," he sighed. "And you must do better than 'try'."

She shot him a glare from between her lashes. "Well, it's the best I can do. And you ought to be glad one of us is willing to see reason. You certainly aren't."

His grip tightened until it verged on painful. "You will cease to taunt me. You will beg my pardon."

"I will not."

"Then you will not eat."

"Fine," she snarled. "I was getting tired of the local diet anyway." Then she slumped in sudden depression. "Oh, who am I kidding? This is never going to work. Not for a minute. Not for a day. Erik, you're just going to have to accept that I'm not cut out for this love slave bit. It's tempting, I admit. You're gorgeous. You're sexy. You do things to me that are almost worth everything else in this rotten time. But I don't belong here, and I have to go home."

Her words seemed to reverberate in his head. She would go home. She would leave him. A haunting emptiness flooded his soul at the thought. And fear. She had no more thought for the consequences of her actions than did Harold. She was indeed defiant enough to run from him.

It chilled him. With her beauty, she could never hope to escape notice. Any woman alone was vulnerable. One without possessions of any kind was even more so. She could never hope to buy protection. She would be captured and she would suffer far worse than hunger. As would he, for that matter.

"Lorelei, you will not escape me," he informed her. "You would be found and used, even killed. I have seen a woman raped to death."

That sobered her, he noted with satisfaction. Indeed, she looked ill.

"Then would I have to kill the men responsible. Then would I be outlawed for murder, as the death of a slave is of no consequence, especially one who has run away. Then would we both end miserably," he finished in a grim voice.

"Oh." Her voice sounded very small.

He had succeeded in making his reasoning known. He had succeeded in frightening her. But he could not hope the lesson would be remembered. She would forget, and he could not bear to think of the consequences.

She belonged to him. He could not avoid his duty. He would see to her protection, though doubtless she would have a sudden desire to swim again.

When he spoke again, his voice held the finality of his decision. "You will obey me. You will have no choice."

She looked distinctly displeased. "Why not?"

She should have known better than to ask.

Lorelei looked back down at herself and sighed. Pitiful. No, worse than that. She looked ridiculous. If any paparazzi saw her like this, she'd be the laughingstock of the whole music world for the rest of her life.

Harold, of course, thought it was hilarious. He kept looking at her and breaking into fresh bursts of laughter.

She was going to kill him when she got loose.

Meanwhile, she pretended not to notice the way the entire crew was enjoying the floor show she was unintentionally providing. At least Erik had relented enough to dress her in his shirt first. Although it probably owed more to his own jealousy than to any concern for her feelings. He wasn't trying to spare her any embarrassment. He was doing this for no other reason than to humiliate her. Still, at least she was tied up wearing a shirt that was practically a dress on her instead of stark naked.

Erik was keeping her tied hand and foot and on a leash. He had her right where he wanted her. And he was right. She didn't have any choice but to do what she was told. If he said "come" and pulled the leash, she could go willingly or she could get dragged. When he wanted her to stay put, he tied her to the spot he wanted her in.

The rope didn't even allow her enough freedom of movement to practice tai chi. She could just take baby steps. And the gag kept her from even singing to entertain herself.

Lorelei was bored, uncomfortable, restless, irritated and aching to get even with a certain cold-blooded, heartless excuse for a Norseman. Not only did he keep her tied up, he wasn't going to let her eat until she apologized, and the more time went on, the more her anger solidified into stubborn immovability.

As a result, she was on a hunger strike to rival Ghandi.

Not that Erik noticed. He didn't even look her way. He just went about his business, sailed, and generally did what Vikings do without seeming to notice that he had a slave on a rope. That had to be hard to do when she was never more than a few feet from him, day or night.

Thinking of the nights, she ground her teeth in helpless fury. Master Erik continued his silent insistence that she share his bed each and every night, in spite of the fact that she wasn't talking to him. Although it was possible he didn't know that she wasn't talking to him, since the gag remained in place unless he was letting her drink.

To give him some credit, he didn't touch her sexually. Still, she could hardly have stopped him if he'd tried, and that was infuriating. And for all she knew, he looked at it as more punishment. Withholding orgasms *and* food to discipline the slave. Well, she'd show him. It'd be a cold day in hell before she'd apologize to him for anything.

Since she had nothing better to do, she settled down to sulk as if it was an art form she wanted to master.

Chapter Nine

"How long will you continue this?" Harold inquired.

Erik had no need to ask what was meant. He had no need to hear his brother's nagging on the subject, either. Bad enough that he had Lorelei always behind him like a silent reproach. She was angry. She was also more stubborn than he would have believed. Had he guessed the depth of her willfulness, he would have chosen a different method to impress the need for obedience upon her. He had thought she would repent within a few hours. Instead it dragged out, an endless torment to both of them.

Every night, he asked her if she would retract her insolent speech. Every night she said the same phrase in reply. The words were unknown to him, but the meaning was clear. He replaced the gag each time without another word, but Harold was correct. It could not continue.

For three days, she had eaten nothing and his little slave was not a large woman. Each night while she slept he felt her ribs grow more prominent. He listened to her shallow breathing. He heard the growling of her aching belly. The discipline meant to teach her a lesson was torturing him, instead. And he was growing hungry himself. He had found the first day that he could not eat knowing she went hungry. Erik scowled at the thought and ignored his brother in hopes that he would take the hint and make himself scarce.

"At first, I found it entertaining to watch the two of you do battle," Harold continued when Erik made no reply. "But of late, you cease to amuse me. She has not tried to jump overboard in days. You do not even let her tell stories. You keep her bound and gagged, and what sport is there in that?"

When Erik continued to ignore him, Harold stepped before him to block his view and force him to pay attention.

"Sell her to me," the younger man suggested. "Obviously she displeases you. Why keep her if she is so much trouble? Sell her to me. I enjoy her fantastic tales of the future."

Erik reminded himself that this was his brother. That there was nothing between his brother and his woman. Did he not have the proof of that? Perhaps he should sell her. Then would she eat, and if she found trouble as she seemed determined to do, it would be on Harold's head and not his own.

Then he thought of the two of them together. She was a beautiful woman, Harold, a man of lusty appetites. He would want her. What man would not? An image rose in his mind. She lay pale and nude beneath his brother, who was panting and thrusting...

It took the combined efforts of Svein and Bjarni to break Erik's grip on Harold's throat.

"I believe that is a 'no'," Harold remarked hoarsely when he could speak.

"Your quickness of mind astounds me," Erik growled. "She is mine. You will not speak of this again."

Harold looked wounded at the very thought. "Would I do such a thing? I asked. You refused. The matter ends there."

Erik scowled even more blackly at that disclaimer. Then his gaze settled on Lorelei. She was too quiet. She had not glared at him all morning, now that he considered it. She had not wanted to get up, either, but he had reached his limit of endurance. He could have remained abed with her and eased his need, or he could have risen. He had chosen to rise.

He found that he missed her spitting fury. Indeed, this stillness was most alarming. Almost without conscious thought, his steps brought him to her. Erik knelt to untie her and wrapped the end around his hand. Still, she didn't stir.

"Come," he said gently, giving her lead a tug.

She remained rooted in place with her knees drawn up to her chest. Freya, now what was he to do? Drag her? She was the most stubborn, willful woman it had ever been his misfortune to meet. Exasperated, he grasped her shoulders and pulled her to her feet.

Her eyes met his, and the misery he read there struck him like a blow. Then she closed her eyes and slid back down to the deck.

"Come," Erik repeated. He lifted her easily and carried her to the enclosed hold. She felt warm to his touch, and a frown creased his brow. "Woman, are you ill?"

She failed to answer, and with impatient hands he removed the gag and bonds. Free, she remained silent and turned to curl on her side.

"You are angry," he stated. No response. He sat beside her and lifted her into his lap. She did not resist. Neither did she seem to welcome his touch. Erik sighed and stroked the smooth length of her hair.

She had been so still that he was unprepared for her sudden action. She slid one of his armbands free, rolled from him and stood in a single, fluid motion while she slipped the heavy ring up her own arm.

He waited. Finally, he asked, "If I give you one of your own, would that please you?"

She stood like a statue for a long moment, staring wordlessly at him. Her eyes went from him, to the armband she'd snatched, back to him. Then they filled with tears.

"No," she whispered. "I don't understand. Why didn't it work?"

She stared at the stupid piece of metal in disbelief. It hadn't worked. She wasn't home. She was stuck. She started to sob in mixed disappointment, rage, and despair. When Erik's arms closed around her, she leaned into him and cried harder. "I want to go home," she wailed.

"This I know."

"It didn't work. Why didn't it work?"

Erik didn't answer that one. Not that she expected him to. How was he supposed to know why she had a broken time-travel object? Maybe it was only good for a one-way ticket. Maybe she was stuck there for good.

When she quieted down, he was still holding her, rocking her in his lap and whispering soothing nonsense words. She sniffled loudly and let him comfort her. At least he did that much. He seemed to know how, too. He rubbed her back, stroked her hair and cradled her head against his chest as if he understood that she just wanted to burrow in and not face anyone. Especially anyone she was mad at. Like him.

"What did not work?" Erik inquired after a while.

"The armband," she answered dispiritedly. "I thought it would work the same way going back, but it didn't. Or maybe I did something the first time that made a difference." She straightened up, inspired by that thought. "Now there's an idea. Maybe I didn't exactly recreate the circumstances. Although I can hardly produce a rock concert in the background for atmosphere." She put her dark head back on his shoulder and mulled it over. "Or here's an idea. I remember this Star Trek episode that had a sequence of tones that triggered a door.

Captain Kirk opened it by accident the first time when he pulled out his communicator. Maybe it has a musical key."

She hummed experimentally. Then she paused. "If that's it, though, I could probably spend the next ten years trying variations of combinations and still not come up with the right one. Can I keep your armband that long?"

He smoothed her hair back and kissed the crown of her head. "You may have one like it, but if you intend to return to your people I will stop you."

Lorelei tilted her face up to meet his eyes. "Why? Aren't you sick of this yet?"

"I tire of this foolishness between us. Of you, never."

"Well, it's bound to happen." She curled more securely into his lap. "Just think about it. Since you're so fond of little proverbs, maybe this one will get through to you. A bird and a fish may fall in love, but where will they live?"

Erik frowned at the bleak tone. "You are not a bird, you are a woman. And I am a man, not a fish."

"Thank you, Mr. Literal."

"Erik," he corrected her.

"I knew that."

Irritation colored her voice. He found it a curious relief in contrast to the uncharacteristic hopelessness when she spoke of birds and fishes. She would cease to think of running away. She would cease to think they did not belong together. She would accept her new life. She would accept him.

Fierce possessiveness seized him, combined with a yearning he could not even put a name to. He pleased her. That she was angry with him mattered not at all. She could not deny that he pleased her as well as she pleased him.

Her stomach growled audibly just then.

"Little one, you will cease your stubbornness," he informed her.

"Thank you, but I'm not nearly hungry enough to eat a helping of crow."

"Again you speak of birds. Enough. You will eat."

"I'm not apologizing. I didn't do anything to apologize for. I'm not sorry, and I'm not going to say I am, either," Lorelei snapped in response.

Erik nodded in acknowledgement. "This I believe."

She gave him a suspicious look. "If I didn't know better, I'd think you were making a heavy-handed attempt at being funny."

"My hands are as they always are. You are trying to change the subject. I have had enough of your stubbornness. You will eat, and I will hear no argument."

"Well, I'm still not—"

Erik cut her off in the middle of her indignant response by placing one of the hands she accused of heaviness over her mouth. Then he gave her a gentle shake. "No more," he said softly. "I will find some other way to teach you what you must learn. You will eat because I cannot watch you suffer any longer, and you may speak and move freely if you will stay in my sight."

She blinked in surprise. "Really?"

A slight smile touched his mouth. "Do you find it so surprising that your unhappiness displeases me?"

She gave him an arch look. "Don't try to convince me that you have a heart. You just want my body."

In answer, he slid his hands along her waist, up her ribcage to cup her breasts. "This I admit," he growled. "Your body pleases me." His fingers stroked, kneaded and rubbed in a way that communicated that truth very clearly. "I want your body, yes." Then he released her and slid reluctant hands back down to her waist. "But not when you are fainting. Eat. Walk about. Tell Harold some of your wondrous lies. And if you feel unwell, you will get out of the sun and rest."

She looked confused.

Erik cupped her cheek and frowned again at the flush of heat. "Do your people not have sun? You look unused to it. The sun is stronger on the water, Lorelei. In the south countries the sun does not last all day in the summer. You must be from far away. Take care to grow accustomed to it gradually."

She smiled at him. "You know something? You can be kind of sweet, in a macho, barbarian kind of way."

He knew he should chide her for speaking disrespectfully.

But instead he smiled back. Then he kissed her. "You, also, are sweet," he breathed against the incredible sweetness of her mouth. He drew back as if to let her go, then claimed her lips again hungrily. When he released her, he told her, "I have missed your sweetness."

Her eyes were wide and filled with a sparkle instead of sparks. "Wow," she murmured. "Maybe abstinence makes the heart grow fonder." Then she burst into laughter.

For once, he could not bring himself to object that she made sport of him. It pleased him too much to hear her laugh.

She handed the armband back, and he took it wordlessly.

"Erik, have you ever noticed the links on that design seeming to move?"

In the process of sliding it back into place, Erik paused and gave her a cautious look. She was not serious, was she? Had he not determined that she was as sound of mind as he was himself? Her gaze was focused on the entwined figure decorating his armband and her smooth brows drew together in a slight frown of concentration. She did indeed appear serious.

She had spoken of his armband from the very first, now that he considered it. She had claimed that Harold had given it to her, only then she had decided that it was not Harold after all, nor his armband. She had also seemed truly surprised when she took it and nothing had happened.

An uneasy thought stirred. Could there be some truth to her wild tales? Could she in fact be a traveler from the distant future? But if so, what possible importance did a piece of jewelry hold?

None, he decided firmly. She was merely telling her tales again and attempting to throw him off of the subject of how she intended to escape him. Not that she would succeed. He hid a smile with difficulty at the thought. She was proving a continual challenge, and he looked forward to thwarting whatever plot she concocted.

Oddly enough, he found her pleasing in spite of her defiance and stubbornness. He had envisioned a less contentious relationship. One that would provide him with a peaceful area of calm in the storm of life, much as eddies of calm could be found beside a rushing current. Instead, he had found an undertow.

She did not care if she angered him. She made no effort to exert her wiles to sway him. She did have some caution, but no fear of him, and that amazed him. Did she not realize the power he held over her life? He could keep her for himself, or order her to service every man on board his longboat and she would have no choice in the matter. He could give her away or sell her and she would have to go. He could beat or otherwise abuse her. Not that he would do so. But she belonged to him and his ownership was absolute. Why did she seem unconcerned?

Or was she unconcerned? He frowned slightly. She had spoken wildly of losing herself to him. Of being overpowered and taken until nothing remained. He had thought at the time that her fear was a physical one, that his size and strength alarmed her. Physical injury was a reasonable concern. If he failed to control himself or acted without thought for her, she could be badly hurt without his intending it. Then he had found her untouched and believed her fear to be a mixture of ignorance and womanly feeling.

She had wanted to wash away the evidence of his touch. He had hurt her feelings. He was still not entirely certain why, but he had no wish to do so again. Yet he could not put her wishes or her feelings above his duty.

She had said that she did not mind his touch. That she had no objection to sharing his bed. But she had also spoken of ugliness and being kicked out of paradise, which he took to mean a place like Valhalla and perhaps the same one the Christians spoke of.

Erik sighed inwardly. The woman was a mass of confusion and there was no understanding her. No wonder he had thought her mad. He would become mad himself if he tried to understand the tangled workings of her mind.

"Lorelei," he said calmly, "the figure is made of metal. It is not alive. It is made from—"

"Silver and gold, right, I know," she interrupted. "Still, there's something funny about it." She traced the outline again, then continued, "When I put it on, not just now, but the first time, I could swear that it started moving."

She fell silent for a moment. "Maybe it was just a trick of the light," she muttered.

Erik took her hand and placed it against his chest. "Enough of your tales. You have delayed for too long. I find I have had too much of abstinence."

Lorelei gave him a lazy smile. "Oh? What did you have in mind?"

He gave a low growl in answer. Then he pulled her slight form on top of himself and claimed her mouth in a deep, drugging kiss. He tugged her hips over his and pushed her knees to the outside of his thighs, forcing her to straddle him and mold him with her womanly cradle.

She melted against him with a soft sound of approval and encouragement, arching the small of her back slightly so that her hardened nipples teased his chest through the fabric of his shirt.

He slid his hands below the hem and pushed it up to her hips. His hands stroked the tempting curve of her buttocks, then came around and moved higher to cup and lift the soft peaks that tempted him. His thumbs grazed her hardened, pebbled nipples and he was rewarded with a moan of pleasure at the caress.

"So you like that?" Erik asked huskily against her lips.

"Oh, yes. Are you kidding? You're wonderful," she informed him. He could feel her breasts swelling and tightening in his hands and her responsiveness sent a rush of urgent heat through him.

No longer content with the soft feminine weight filling his hands, Erik released the twin globes and moved lower. One palm lifted her belly slightly. The other moved between her thighs to seek out her feminine core.

The slickness that he found made him want to spill his seed then and there. She was wet and welcoming. He was unable to resist testing her readiness, but the sensation of her slick heat closed tightly around his finger drove him to a fever pitch of need. He withdrew, raised her long enough to free himself, and then he was burying his shaft in her. She took him inside herself, and he groaned again at the pleasure of filling her tight channel.

He felt her clenching and rippling around him and the knowledge that she had found her pleasure when he had barely entered her sent him over the edge himself. He ended it with one hard thrust that seated him fully inside her. Then he spilled himself endlessly into her, his bruising grip on her hips holding her in place as she writhed in spasm after spasm of ecstasy.

Afterwards, he slowly relaxed his hold and wrapped his arms around her. She slipped her hands beneath his neck and cuddled willingly. "Erik," she whispered. "God."

He smiled, although she could not see it with her face buried against his chest. "Erik is enough. Master if you insist on a title."

She sank her teeth into the nearest muscle in response. "Funny. Very funny."

He laughed at her irritation.

She leaned up to frown at him.

Then she smiled and kissed him instead. "Oh, go ahead and laugh. I just had a multiple orgasm. Or at least I think that's what it was. Whatever you want to call it, it felt terrific. I'm too happy to fight with you." Lorelei settled back into his arms and spread kisses along the column of his throat. "Erik, that was amazing. Can we do it again?"

Her eagerness made him laugh again. "Woman, I have just spent myself. You milked me of all my seed. I may not have the strength to lay you again this evening."

"Oh." She tightened around him experimentally, since he was still inside her. "Are you sure?"

"I am sure. I am sure you are going to drive me to madness," he informed her. "But I will promise you this, if you have need and I have not recovered, I will see to you."

She raised her head again, her eyes filled with silent curiosity.

"Like this," he explained. He shifted her so that they lay side by side. His hand moved over her plundered mound, stroking the length of her. He settled his thumb below her nub and lazily circled it while his fingertips stroked in and out of her opening. She made a low sound of surprise. Erik smiled at her, liking the way desire made her face flush and her green eyes darken like the sea before a storm.

"And this," he breathed. He widened her and slid two fingers inside. She gasped. He increased the pressure with his thumb and teased her sensitized opening with a third finger, slipping in and out rapidly.

She shuddered and spasmed around his finger in a liquid rush.

Incredibly, her desire and her response to him had him rock hard again when he would have sworn it was impossible. Watching her face while he brought her to pleasure made him want her again with aching intensity.

He rolled her to her back, stripped away the shirt to bare her fully against him and drove inside her in one swift movement.

"Erik," she gasped. He felt her shuddering in his arms and felt the powerful, purely male satisfaction of conquest.

"Rub your breasts against me," he commanded in a low growl.

She did, arching into him in a motion that opened her hips even more and brought him more fully inside. She made a sharp sound of surprise.

He rode her with ruthless strength, driving deeply into her again and again. She was soft and wet enough, ready enough not to feel any hurt. He could take her with brutal force, she was so ready. He took her with driving fury, making her keen with pleasure as he buried himself full length in her. Then he shuddered in a violent spending and knew he planted his seed deep within her virgin womb.

She was asleep when he recovered. Erik levered himself above her and watched her face for some time. A slight smile curved her lips, and her lashes fanned against the delicate skin beneath her eyes. It looked faintly bruised and he touched it gently. She had not slept well of late, it seemed. It pleased him that she slept deeply now after serving his need so well.

He palmed one breast in a purely possessive hold, liking the silky feel of her skin and the freedom to touch and take as he would. Even in sleep she responded to him. She turned towards his touch and made a soft sound of sleepy satisfaction when he gathered her against his side. He held her until he knew she would not wake when he left her. He tucked the lynx skin around her and kissed the rosy crest of one breast for no other reason than that it pleased him to do so before he dressed and went to check the course once more.

Chapter Ten

There was a campfire in a forest clearing. Lorelei could see a man sitting by the fire with two large dogs, one on each side of him. She walked towards the trio and when she got closer, she realized the animals weren't dogs at all. They were wolves. The man turned his head towards her. Firelight showed a patch covering one eye.

A man with one eye and two wolves could only be..."Odin."

He smiled. "That name will do."

Lorelei waved her hands in the air, too exasperated to be still. Even her damn dreams were full of riddles. Was it too much to hope for an escape when she closed her eyes?

"What next? Armbands that come alive when you don't expect them to and don't when you do expect it, Vikings, a Norse god and guardian wolves. Could this get any weirder?"

"That's possible. You should be careful what you wish for."

She stared at him. "What I wish for? What do you mean?"

He didn't answer her. Instead, he asked another question. "What do you know of the Rhinegold?"

"Like in the story? Well, for starters, the ring made nine more of itself every..." Lorelei trailed off as an idea came to her that was completely outrageous. But then, not any more outrageous than having a fire lit conversation with an embodied myth. "You're not telling me that some of the replicas got loose and you lost track of them?"

"I keep my eye on them."

He was serious. Lorelei stared at him in disbelief, but there was no hint of humor in his face. "The designs in Erik's armbands were made from a piece of the Rhinegold?"

Well, that made as much sense as anything else in this crazy dream. As much sense as anything else in her current waking life, actually. "And if they are, why aren't weird things happening to *him*?" Why hadn't anything happened to her when she'd taken one and put it on earlier, for that matter?

"By themselves they are inert. The wearer must have the key."

"I don't have any key!" Lorelei burst out. As she'd proven in her failed attempt to get back home.

"Don't you?" Odin stood up and turned to face her fully. He rested one hand on each of the wolves' heads as he spoke. "Be careful what you wish for."

Then the trio and the fire all vanished, leaving her alone in the dark forest clearing under a starless sky.

Lorelei woke to a feeling of delicious lassitude that lasted until she stretched. Immediately, abused muscles protested and various aches and minor discomforts made themselves known. That brought her firmly into the present moment and cleared away the remnants of her dream. She'd heard rumors that people on ships had bizarre dreams and apparently that was true because she'd had some doozies lately.

She grimaced at both the memory of the dream and her aching body. The sex had been amazing. So there was a price to pay for all that skyrocketing passion. She might have known. She felt raw, sore and bruised. Still, a silly smile stole over her face at the memory of the afternoon spent kissing and making up with Erik.

He was wonderful. He made her hot and eager for his touch, when every other man she'd known had left her cold at the first hint of a sexual overture. The smile widened as she pictured the tabloid headline, "A Viking Took My Virginity". A sub-heading would read, "Siren rocker no longer frigid". She laughed out loud at the image, then groaned when she moved.

"You sound pleased, yet I think we may have overdone it."

She started at Erik's voice and then turned her head to find him by the door. "Hello, lover. Come and kiss me. Then help me get up, I don't think I can stand after what you did to me. Not that I'm complaining," she added hastily, with a lopsided grin. "And maybe it just seems like overdoing it because I'm such a novice. I might just need more practice."

He laughed at her enthusiastic suggestion and came to lift her easily to her feet.

"I think you will wait for further practice," he informed her. He smoothed her hair back and frowned at the reddened, abraded skin on her face and neck from his beard. "How badly do you hurt?"

"It only hurts when I laugh." Her eyes sparkled with remembered delight. "And when I move. Erik, you've crippled me." She wrapped her arms around his waist and leaned against him in trusting abandon. "It was the most wonderful experience in my life. I take it back. I like your time." Happiness bubbled in her sultry voice.

He hugged her and swung her up in his arms. "I hope you have no urgent need to wash away my touch this time, but a bath may help the soreness."

She leaned her head against his shoulder. "Hm. Nice thought. Except I'm not sure about the idea of putting saltwater on my wounds."

He gave her a thoughtful look. "Then I must say this a less tactful way. Woman, you stink."

"I probably do," she agreed cheerfully.

He had her nearly to the door before she realized she didn't have anything on, and neither did he. "Erik, wait! We can't go out there like this!"

He didn't hesitate. "Do not concern yourself. Nobody will look."

To her surprise, he was right. He must have forewarned the others that he was giving his crazy slave a bath. A bucket of water and a bar of soap waited.

"Oh, Erik, you really are a sweet man." She gave him a smile, slipped free, grabbed the soap and made use of it.

Minutes later they were rinsed clean and headed back for dry clothes. At least, she hoped she got clothes. She peeked at her bearded Norseman, searching for a clue as to his intentions.

He caught her look, and to her surprise, looked slightly apologetic. "The saltwater stings, I know. But you will have fresh water to bathe in come morning."

She halted in surprise. "Fresh water? Really? Then we're almost where we're going?"

He caught her around the waist and pulled her along, guiding her back to the cargo hold and searching out another shirt for her to wear. "Really." He dropped the garment over her head and tugged it into place.

"And where are we going?" Lorelei asked, curious.

"Home."

"Home." She shot him an exasperated look, but he was already turning away to dress himself. "Could you be a little more informative? Where is home?"

"A farm on a fjord."

She ground her teeth in frustration. "Of course. A fjord. Where else would a Viking live? I should have known."

He gave her an even stare. "Home is where I say it is."

"Oh, not the master-slave bit again," she protested. "All right, all right," she added when he started towards her. "I said I'd be reasonable, and I meant it. I'll toe the line. You may find this hard to believe, but I have no desire to find myself on the wrong side of your law. I'll do my best to be obedient."

"You are right, I find this hard to believe," he grumbled, looking suspicious.

She gave him a winning smile. "Don't worry. I'll get the hang of it, for as long as I need to. It isn't like I have to play slave girl forever."

The suspicion in his face hardened into resolution and she got the distinct feeling that she'd said something wrong. "Uh, Erik?"

He didn't answer. He just kept coming towards her. Nervous, she backed away until he had her pinned against the wall. He lifted her and spread her legs to stand between them, holding her up with his body. "You are my property," he informed her. "Do you understand? This is no game. I could take you now, and you would have no choice but to submit."

"Really?" Deceptive innocence sweetened her voice. She could get free if she wanted to. He didn't know her weird workout was a form of self-defense. She thought about giving her little secret away and decided not to if she could avoid it. If it ever came to a real fight with him, she'd need the edge surprise would give her. She went with her instincts instead, trusting that she was right. He didn't want to hurt her, and he knew she was too sore to find sex anything but painful just then.

"Okay, have it your way. I'll probably cry the whole time, and I won't be able to crawl, let alone walk afterwards, but you're bigger and stronger." She heaped guilt on his head and laid it on as thick as she dared. "You'll probably tear me, too. I'm too dry. I might bleed. It could take days or even weeks to heal, and you'd have to find someone else to screw, but you probably have enough slaves not to be too inconvenienced."

He muttered curses against her hair, then lifted her to eye level. "Woman, cease your mockery. You tempt me to prove my point. Your pain would be small compared to what you invite with your endless taunting."

"Erik, I said I'd behave. Either you believe me or you don't, but don't threaten me." She glared back at him, furious that he could be so callous after the tenderness he'd shown her. "If you're going to do it, then get it over with. But when you're finished, don't ever touch me again or I'll fight you with every ounce of strength in my body. And I'll hate you forever."

"Forever is a long time."

"Not as long as you might think. But if you insist on putting a limit on it, I'll hate you for a thousand years." As Lorelei spoke, the words came with a force that surprised her. She felt like she'd just given voice to an ancient curse. The words held the same power she used to sway a crowd during a concert to create the mood she desired, the nameless force that she shaped with her vocal cords and gave heightened structure to with musical composition.

Be careful what you wish for...

The dream warning came back to her in a rush and cold panic flooded her body. What if she catapulted back into the future right now? She would lose him forever. And as angry as he made her, as fiercely as they fought, she couldn't bear the thought of never seeing him again.

"I didn't mean it!" she yelled and threw her arms and legs around Erik, clinging to him with all her strength. "I take it back! Erik, don't let me go!"

He stared down at her, not knowing what to make of her. One moment she defied him and vowed her hatred, the next she clung to him as if she couldn't bear any separation.

Words continued to spill out of her as she clutched him tighter. "I don't know how the damn things work. What if they send me back right now? Like that movie with Christopher Reeve. He goes back in time and meets the perfect woman and they fall in love, and then he puts his hand in his pocket and touches a coin. Bam, he's yanked back to his own time. And that's it, they lost each other forever! What if it happened like that to us?"

She made no sense. But she was truly distraught. Erik frowned and wondered how he could calm her fears when there was no reason to them.

Moments before, he had been intent on carrying out his duty to teach her a lesson. The seriousness of her situation seemed to elude her. She treated her position as his slave as if it were a jest, something she could abide by or discard as it suited her. If it were only the two of them, she could do as she pleased. But at home, she would bear the full penalty of the law and her defiance of it would be no laughing matter. And now he wanted only to comfort her and take away her fear.

But he had a duty, his mind protested. Was he to turn his back on his duty for her? His father was jarl. He had a duty to abide by the law and to see that all those under his responsibility did so as well. Better she suffer some discomfort now than the agony of real punishment that her insolence and refusal to acknowledge her enslaved state invited. He would spare her that.

He remembered her voice, low and shaking with anger. *"I will hate you for a thousand years."*

He had never before failed his duty. But he could not help the feeling, in spite of all logical reason, that he was failing her. He had thought to have her and fulfill his duty too. But as the days wore on and she failed to accept her role, his duty and his desire fought a war within him. If duty lay one way and his heart another, how was he to choose and keep his honor?

One thing was certain. He lacked the will to let her go, even if he could be certain her freedom would not mean her demise.

He sighed and wrapped his arms around her, cradling her close. "You need have no fear of losing me."

She was shaking in his embrace. "How do you know? You don't have any better idea of how I got here than I do. One minute I'm getting ready to go on stage and the next I'm in front of you and you're buying me at sword point. If we don't know how that happened, how do we know it won't just happen again? The dream said be careful what I wish for, that I have the key. What if I got so mad that I wished I'd never met you and it happened?"

She ended her outburst in tears and huddled into his chest, crying as if her world was ending. It tore at his heart. Her fear was real even if the reason for it escaped him.

"You will not lose me." He held her firmly between himself and the wall, his arms holding her tightly, his body bracing hers, only the fabric of the shirt she wore separating them.

"It could happen," she insisted. She twisted in his arms, yanking the shirt up to press her bare skin against his. With her legs locked around his waist, his hard shaft rode between her spread thighs, grazing her moist womanly cleft. "I want you inside me. Right now. Hard." She clawed at him and fought to align them better, to force his flesh into hers.

"You said you were too sore. You would find no pleasure in it," he rasped back.

"I don't care!" She fought to move in his embrace, to get closer.

"You will care later." He struggled for control, for the strength to resist her, but she was positioned too perfectly and her slick woman's flesh was already enclosing the head of him.

It took only a slight shift of angle as he tilted his pelvis to enter her partway. He heard her breath catch and knew that in spite of her demands, she was too unready to take him like this.

He slid one hand between them and found the swollen bud nestled in her woman's flesh with his finger. He stroked the sensitized nub until he felt the tight channel that clenched at him growing wetter, prepared for his entry. He thrust deep and slid all the way inside and then stopped, feeling her clutching at him from without and within. It undid him. He withdrew his hand and slid it over her hip and cupped her bare, rounded buttocks with both hands. Then he withdrew partway, only to thrust back into her again and again with a force that she should have protested. Comforting her in the only way she would allow. Proving that he was there, that she was his, making her forget her fear of losing him in the endless mating of their flesh.

Afterwards he carried her back to the bed of furs they shared, still buried deep inside her, making her moan with pleasure at every step. He lowered her down until her back rested against the fur and his body covered hers. His weight drove him further into her and she sighed.

He knew he should withdraw from her. Yet he had no will to leave her body and allow her to recover. He wanted to remain inside her for as long as it gave her comfort. He understood his little slave more and more, understood that she needed the proof of his possession and that words alone would not have reached her. He only hoped she would not suffer much discomfort later.

Erik waited until the tremors had left her body and her breath had settled into a calmer pattern. Then he withdrew from her and stood, looking down at her. Her eyes met his. She looked confused and a little shocked. He wanted to gather her up in his arms and comfort her. He wanted more to put some distance between them and the growing tension in his world that she was the cause of. In silence, he bound her hands and hobbled her feet once more. Then he left her without a word, not trusting himself to speak.

When he passed Harold, he muttered, "See to her." He could not do so himself, but with his brother for company she would lack for nothing and would not be alone with any fear that still haunted her.

When Harold appeared, Lorelei would have liked to disappear, preferably into a large, deep hole in the ground. The large, loose shirt Erik had dressed her in before they both lost their minds covered her decently, but it was obvious what they'd been doing. Going at it as violently as they argued.

He didn't give her a chance to be embarrassed, though. Simply helped her up and led her out to look at the water. When he offered her something to eat, she took it without looking and ate it without comment. She wasn't hungry. It tasted like sawdust. But she knew she needed to eat, so she went through the motions.

He gave her some mysterious liquid and she drank it thirstily. It burned all the way down, but not unpleasantly. They sat together for some time in silence, drinking and looking out at the sea. After a while, Lorelei suggested, "Sing me one of your songs."

He was happy to oblige, and Lorelei leaned back and listened to the rhythmic chant. After a while, she recognized what he was singing.

About a thousand years later, the story would be retold by Wagner in music, Tolkien in literature. Harold was singing part of the Ring Cycle.

Loki had stolen the ring of Rhinegold from the dwarf Andarvi, and now Odin must recover it from the lair of a dragon to save nine worlds from disaster.

She listened with rapt attention, closing her eyes to hear better. As a musician, she'd learned to listen with total concentration, blocking out all distractions in order to isolate and analyze the parts of a composition. As a result, she could remember and play anything after she'd heard it once. Now she listened intently to the old Nordic myth, and wondered that she could hear it told by an actual Norseman. It wasn't every day a student of mythology got a chance like that.

Harold sang of the power of the ring and she shivered.

The design in Erik's armbands were made with gold.

Her eyes flew open and she considered the wild possibility for a moment.

It was just a story. Her dream was just a stupid dream. She had an overactive imagination, that was all. Erik's armbands were real, while the one Loki stole was not. There couldn't be any connection whatsoever between them. And even if there was, she couldn't control the armbands. She didn't have the power.

Lorelei pushed the subject to the back of her mind and concentrated on the saga. Now Harold was singing of the Volsungs, the guardian wolves of Valhalla. She forced herself to pay attention. She might not get a chance like this again. All in all, her Viking vacation was proving quite an opportunity.

Her relationship with Erik might be a hopeless tangle, but nobody had done anything to hurt her. Harold was doing his best to be a friend to her, and considering the Nordic theme of family loyalty and honor that cropped up repeatedly in their myths, that was no small thing.

She ought to be more appreciative.

But she was too emotionally drained, or maybe too drunk, to feel much of anything just then.

Harold got to the part about the marriage of Siggier of Hafvang to the Volsung Signy, and stopped.

She looked up expectantly.

"No more tonight," he saidwith a smile. "My throat grows too dry."

"Oh." She smiled back at him and passed the booze. They drank in silence for a while longer. Then Lorelei roused herself to ask a question that had been bothering her. "Harold, I have to know something. You guys don't have sonar or radar or anything like that. I don't think you even have compasses yet. So how do you know where you are?"

The big man frowned at her. "I do not understand your meaning."

"I mean, how do you know where you are in relation to land? How do you keep from getting lost at sea?"

"Oh, that." Harold waved a dismissive hand and drank again. "Many things. The color of the water, for one."

She sat bolt upright and stared at him, amazed. "You're kidding."

"No. The polar current is green, and can be easily seen."

"You're kidding," Lorelei said again.

"You grow drunk," Haroldsaid. "Have some more."

"Thank you, I will." She took another drink and noted that after a while it stopped burning and she just felt warm all over. "What else do you use?"

"A sunstone, with a dial and pointer."

She frowned at Harold. "A sunstone? What's that?"

"A rock."

"A rock," she repeated numbly. "For navigation?"

"It changes color, also," Harold explained.

She took another drink to brace herself. "It changes color. A rock. And the water changes color." She started to laugh. "I'm trapped in the ancient past with a band of Vikings who navigate the open sea by colors. Colors!" she howled, slapping her thigh.

Harold missed the joke, but joined in anyway. "Yes, we are fine navigators," he boasted, laughing.

She laughed harder, until she was too weak to move. Not that it mattered. They were all going to die. They were navigating by trying to see currents in the ocean with the naked eye and holding rocks up to the sun to watch them change color.

She could almost believe there was a Loki, and that he was responsible for her little adventure.

Still smiling at the absurdity of it all, she fell asleep.

The next morning, she regretted the previous night. Not only the drinking, since she had a whopping headache and no coffee or aspirin to chase away her hangover. But she regretted laughing at what she'd considered ludicrously primitive navigation methods. She had to eat her words.

They weren't going to die, wreck the ship or get lost at sea.

They were beaching the longboat at the fjord Erik had mentioned.

She blinked and rubbed her eyes to be sure she wasn't imagining things, but she could still see green fields and lush, primeval forests. Green, everywhere. She might have been in Oz, arriving at the Emerald City.

"We're not in Kansas anymore," Lorelei murmured.

She stood, and rubbed her arms in the morning chill. If this was summer, what was winter like? She surveyed the view moodily. At least it was scenic. There was a crowd of people waiting for them, and depression settled over her. She looked exactly like she could be expected to look, considering recent events, and it didn't make for a stunning first impression. She looked pathetic.

She looked down at herself. She was naked except for Erik's overly large shirt. Her hair was in tangles. She was tied hand and foot.

She looked like a fashion victim. No, it was worse than that.

She looked like a slave.

Chapter Eleven

It should have been a joyous homecoming, Erik reflected morosely. His trip had been highly profitable. Not only had he added to his own wealth, but the men who had joined him in the trading voyage had prospered as well. That was good for the settlement. His father would be pleased. Also, he had kept Harold out of trouble and out of the way. Gunnar's anger should have cooled, and as long as Harold kept away from Gudred, a feud might yet be avoided.

A feud with that family was no small thing. Their father, Sigurd, had been Thorolf's strongest opposer. Thorolf had defeated him and become jarl, but the title remained his so long as his strength was sufficient to rule and lead, and so long as he upheld the law by the force of it. Blood feuds broke out when the law was not upheld, for Vikings would seek vengeance for wrongs against their families. A strong leader meant that peace would be kept and the community would prosper.

Sigurd would not have been a strong leader. His head was too hot, and his son showed every sign of following the father. Erik knew well that some day he would have to confront Gunnar as his father had faced Sigurd. Erik was the strongest warrior. The ablest farmer. The best builder, and the most wealthy trader. When the time came for Thorolf to step down, it would be his duty to take his father's place, and Gunnar was the most likely to oppose his leadership.

He cared not for the thought of assuming the duties of a jarl. He would no longer be free to take extended sailing trips for exploration or trade. He would have even less free time than he did now, with only one farmstead dependent on him. But there was no better man to lead, and he had a duty to his people.

It was doubly regrettable that Harold refused to curb his wildness. He had the wit, strength and cunning to be jarl, and his poetry was envied all along the fjord. He was known for his woman-luck, and luck in a leader counted for much.

Erik scowled blackly. Harold should have been the first-born. Then he may have learned something of the meaning of duty and responsibility. Harold would be the one burdened by duty and parental expectations, and Erik would be free to take his woman and sail far away.

There was a pleasant dream. He would carry Lorelei off and show her the islands he had discovered. They would swim and laugh together, and she would forget her anger. He would have no need to fear the penalties of the law falling on her, so she would be free to do as she pleased.

The thought occurred to him that there was perhaps a way around the difficulty he found himself in. He could free her. As a free woman, it would not matter how defiant and proud she was. She would be admired for it, in fact.

Yes, and if he freed her, she would be gone and unprotected. She had no reason to remain and seemed to take no thought for her own safety. Freya, there was no winning. He could not let her go. He could not keep her.

From the first moment he had found her, he had been trapped in the snare of her beauty. He had touched her as no other man had. He had held her while she slept, wiped away her tears. She belonged to him, and with every touch, every word between them the silken snare tightened. There could be no escape for either of them. He could not let her go, even if it meant her undying hatred, and he feared it might come to that.

He heard the angry words again in his memory, "...*for a thousand years.*"

He had avoided her long enough. It was time to take her to his home and see her settled there. She would have to meet his father. He would have to let it be known that she was his and he would not share her, or some man would think to tumble the lovely new slave during the festivities. There would be a celebration to welcome them home, and the drink would flow for days. Slaves were for the entertainment of any who wished to use them, so long as their owners consented. He would have to make it known that he did not consent or he could find himself in the position of killing a man who had tumbled the wrong wench and becoming an outlaw before he had been home a week.

Life had become so much more complicated since he had acquired her.

Erik strode across the deck and found Lorelei in the same place she had slept in. He wondered briefly if she remembered him coming to sleep beside her. He had pillowed her head on his arm. She had not stirred, or made a sound, and he had risen before she woke. She had looked so very small and fragile in sleep. He had felt the need to hold her, as if he could keep her safe from her fears with his strength.

She still looked fragile. She looked as if she might break apart, and he found himself wishing that she would shout at him instead.

He sighed inwardly. But outwardly, his expression was a calm, implacable mask.

She ignored him, or perhaps did not notice him, until he took her arm. Then she jerked in reaction and turned her head towards him. Her face gave away her every thought, Erik noted.

He could tell the moment she decided against pulling away from his touch. Still, her expression was far from welcoming.

She did not want his touch, but she was learning. It gave him no pleasure to know she wanted him not, but she must learn to submit. A slave could not retaliate. A slave could not strike a freeman even in self-defense. A slave could not behave as a freeman did. It was a grave insult to call a Norseman a slave, one worth killing over. Her free ways would be an insult of that order and he would do what he must to curb her.

He saw her eyes return to the waiting crowd, and it seemed natural to bring her close against his side. "Have no fear," he murmured for her ears alone.

A shiver ran through her slight frame, but she remained silent.

That decided him. He lifted her easily and carried her, sparing her the indignity of hobbling along in his wake. She might be too proud to say so, but she was afraid and even if she was still angry with him, he was familiar.

"Put me down," she snarled, but low enough not to be overheard. "I don't want you touching me."

"I will put you down when I choose," he returned.

She raised her face to glare at him. "Getting a thrill, huh? You like your women unwilling and helpless? Well, I hope you're enjoying this."

In spite of himself, Erik smiled. Her fury was so much easier to deal with than the vulnerable look she'd worn when he'd left her. It was a relief to see her fiery spirit return. "I very much enjoy the feel of you in my arms. I may show you later just how much."

Her eyes widened in pretended awe. "Really, master? You would be so generous with your lowly slave?"

He wanted to frown at her sarcasm, but could not resist teasing her. Instead, his smile broadened into a wickedly sensual promise. "I swear to you, I will be very generous."

"Big of you," Lorelei sneered.

"Someday you may grow to like my size."

That silenced her jibes for a while. It amused him, until it occurred to him that she may not have been jesting about being rent and needing time to heal. There had been nothing gentle in their urgent mating. He had taken care to make her ready. But she was not truly hurt, was she? The thought that she might be disturbed him.

It irritated him to worry over her when there was nothing to be done. He would see to her at the first opportunity, he promised himself. She would be disappointed if she thought to rid herself of his attentions by feigning injury, however.

Concern made his voice harsh when he spoke again. "You will keep silent and obey, do you understand?"

"Sorry," she answered, her tone saying clearly that she was anything but. "I intend to scream until your eardrums bleed and fight like a Valkyrie. Don't say I didn't warn you."

Erik stopped abruptly and spanned her waist, turning her so that he held her facing him at eye level. "I do not speak of matters between the two of us. You said you would fight me, and this I can well believe. You have done nothing else since I bought you," he informed her in some exasperation. "I meant you are to obey before others. I have no wish to take you to meet my father and have you offer him a mortal insult."

She blinked, and he could see the fight draining out of her. "Oh."

"He is jarl," Erik went on. "You will behave. Do you understand?"

"Jarl means he's the head honcho?" Lorelei asked tentatively.

He frowned. "Head what?"

"The boss," she clarified. "El Presidente. Supreme Dictator for Life."

"He is the leader."

"That's what I said. Okay, I'll be good." She gave him a furious look. "Not that you would take my word for it. Maybe you should give me a good beating just in case I'm lying."

Erik sighed heavily and stuffed her under his arm again before continuing on his way. "You tempt me, by Thor, you do. You make me long to throttle you."

She nodded. "It's my winning personality."

"More likely it is your disrespectful speech."

To his surprise, she laughed, a short, dry sound. But still, a laugh. The sound warmed him and when he spoke again, it was with a teasing note. "Spare my father your winning personality, woman."

She turned gleaming eyes to meet his. "I'm saving it all for you," she promised sweetly.

As sweet as a venomous serpent waiting to strike, he could not help thinking.

Then she asked almost wistfully, "Do I have to meet him looking like this? I look like I've been through a twelve car pile-up."

He would not ask what a twelve car pile-up was. It would only give her an excuse to invent more of her tales. "You will go as you are."

"I thought you'd say that."

So, her feminine vanity was suffering. He cocked one brow at her questioningly. "You would prefer to look your best and attract more offers to buy you?"

She looked stunned. "Somebody tried to buy me from you already?"

Erik gave her a cold look that made her subside. "You attract male attention enough without inviting more. You go as you are."

Somebody else wanted to buy her. She really could have done without hearing that. Lorelei thought about reminding him that he had promised not to sell her or give her away, but that would have been pushing it. She also considered pleading, but she couldn't bring herself to do it.

Besides, how did she know she'd be worse off than she was with him? The arrogant beast wasn't satisfied with having fun while it lasted. She'd been perfectly willing to play love games with him. But that wasn't good enough. No, he wanted her to heel, sit up and roll over. He wanted a trained pet, not a woman.

And in the middle of a damn argument, she'd lost her mind and begged him to give her another good, hard bump and grind in case she suddenly found herself back where she'd started. In the future. Where she had everything, except him. And faced with the thought of not having him anymore, she'd panicked.

Maybe everything wasn't perfect between them, but physically it had to be about as perfect as it got. And outside of the mind-blowing sex, Erik was a good man. She'd never met another one who could compare. He took his responsibilities seriously, as if they meant life and death. And in this time, she realized, they probably did. She didn't just lust after his incredible body. She felt safe with him. And something more. As if she'd found something she'd always been looking for. And now that she'd found it, she wanted to hold on and not let go.

She had it bad for her Viking, and there was this one little problem. Like he wanted her for a slave. Well, no relationship was perfect. She'd had to fight for everything else she had in life. Why should this be any different? She'd fight for his heart and she wouldn't give up until he gave it to her. Because she wasn't going to be all moony and mushy over him without the feeling being returned.

It was really horrible to be so vulnerable. To know he had the power to hurt her heart. The power he held over her status was meaningless to her, but in the realm of emotions, in her mind and in her physical inability to resist him, she was so utterly vulnerable to him.

"Stop looking so miserable," he muttered. "All the men may think you find me lacking and offer to compensate you."

Her shudder was entirely unfeigned.

"I meant to tease you," Erik said softly.

"Oh. Well, it wasn't funny," Lorelei answered crossly.

"You could tell me you do not find me lacking," he suggested.

"But I do," she sighed. It was so much easier to fight with him than to get into the dangerous realm of Talking About Their Feelings. "Lacking a brain. Lacking a heart. Lacking—"

"Enough," he interrupted. "Cease your insults and show me your meek obedience."

With that, he dumped her on her feet and continued into the house ahead. It had sort of a Bavarian look, she thought. In a rustic kind of way. Sort of a weird combination of a log cabin and an alpine dwelling. Noticing that he wasn't being followed, Erik turned back and hooked an arm around her waist.

"Come, cease your delaying."

"I'm not delaying," she defended herself. "My feet are tied together. I have to take baby steps."

"Let that be a lesson to you. If you were not so defiant, I would not have to hobble you like a horse."

She gasped in outrage. "A horse?"

He plucked her off her feet again and strode with her into the hall. "You have no liking for the comparison?" His warm breath brushed her ear and made her shiver as he continued, "But it is fitting, is it not? You are made to be ridden."

So she made a great first impression on the jarl by kicking his son's shins repeatedly while yelling a string of insults nobody understood except by the tone, since twenty-first century English didn't exist.

That she carried out the impromptu performance dressed in a flapping shirt that had seen better days with her hair hanging around her in wild tangles somehow added to the image of an untamable shrew. The abbreviated length of rope forcibly shortened the distance her leg could swing and made her kicks less than effectual, but she was undeterred. What she lacked in force, she attempted to make up for in sheer repetition.

Erik could restrain her partially, but she continued to flail away with one free foot until he stomped on the length of rope between her ankles. Effectively trapped by his arms and the rope, she subsided, but continued to glower at him.

It didn't seem to bother him in the least. He was laughing almost too hard to maintain a firm grip on her.

"Well, Erik," a deep, masculine voice filled with mild inquiry began, "What have you brought home with you this time?"

Erik took the precaution of clamping one hand over Lorelei's mouth. "Many things, Father," he answered readily. "We found good trading in Birka and Hedeby."

To her disbelief, he went on to recite the cargo manifest in unbelievable detail as to quality, quantity and profit while his father nodded and listened, as if neither of them were aware of her presence, let alone her continued struggle to escape. When she sank her teeth into the fleshy pad of his finger, Erik paused.

"Be good." It was as much a warning as an admonition.

"And this?" Amused interest warmed Thorolf's eyes.

Erik shook his head in rueful regret. "This I purchased in Hedeby for hack silver. Had I only known then the trouble she brought. That slaver got the best of the bargain by far."

She gasped in outrage, but the sound was muffled.

The older man looked thoughtful. "Well do I appreciate the thoughtfulness of my eldest son, and in truth she may be fair, were she cleaner. But if you meant to make a gift of her to me, I can only trust it was before her nature was known to you. Else I must believe you grow impatient with an old man's leadership and wish to harry me to my grave."

Lorelei fairly seethed at that. The implication that she was not only a lowly slave but a worthless one, one that would drive him to an early death, would have been hard to miss. It was a distinctly unsubtle put-down. She glared at the man, since she couldn't give him an appropriate come-back.

She would have known him as Erik's father anywhere, and not just by the attitude. That family resemblance again. Although his features were leaner and sharper, and he had deep grooves in the corners of his eyes. Not that he was old by any means. She would be surprised if he was much over forty. He had the weathered skin of a man who spent a lot of time in the wind and sun that accentuated wrinkles.

His hair was darker, too, a deep brown sprinkled with gray. Aside from that, his build was similar to his sons, which led her to notice that apparently a Viking didn't lose his muscle tone or run to fat in middle age. He'd probably still be an impressive sight at fifty-five. She could believe he'd still have his sword in his hand when the Grim Reaper came. And considering the strength it must take to swing the heavy swords, that was saying something.

She realized that Erik was answering, and forced herself to pay attention. "I would not wish her on you, Father. This one is truly Loki's get."

She'd get him for that crack, Lorelei promised herself. Call her the daughter of trouble, would he? She'd just show him trouble. Loki was also the trickster. Just for that, she'd come up with some tricks to make him regret ever laying eyes on her.

It did her heart good to dream up vengeful fantasies. It kept her mind off the embarrassing situation she found herself in. The hall looked like a formal gathering area, and even the women cooking and working around the central hearth were better dressed than she was. The Nordic style of dress and decor seemed to run to lots of metal and leather, and it made for an interesting combination of the barbaric and the beautiful. Intricate metalwork and tooling decorated everything. Jewels and precious metals sat in bizarre contrast to the primitive lifestyle. Sort of like her bed of lynx skin and mink on the boat, right alongside the lack of running water. Their culture made for a wild mix of incredible luxury and low technology that was mind-boggling, to say the least.

By one standard, these people wore more sheer wealth than many twenty-first century workers earned in a month. By another, the lowliest apartment dweller had a higher standard of living.

However she looked at it, though, she didn't come out looking favorable in comparison. It was like going to meet the governor in her bathrobe. She could kill Erik for putting her there and then laughing at her.

Until it occurred to her that maybe he had reasons. He'd said something about not wanting her to attract attention. No attention of the admiring, positive kind, apparently. By the sound of the discussion with his father, it could be that the highest honcho had his choice of any pretty new faces. Something to consider. If he didn't want to insult anyone but wasn't about to give up the fun of tormenting her himself, wouldn't it make sense to make her look like less than a desirable prize?

Lorelei thought about that while she looked around the rectangular room, noting that windows evidently weren't a high priority. In the winter when the daylight hours shortened and it got too cold to leave the door open, she could only imagine that the hearth lit the hall. Long benches lined the walls, and long tables ran lengthwise in the center.

She was so intent on taking everything in that it took her by surprise when Erik started to haul her back out the way they'd come in. The audience was over, apparently. He didn't uncover her mouth or loosen his hold, however. Instead, he growled at her, "Is this your good behavior? I find it greatly lacking."

Since she couldn't respond, she settled for biting his hand.

She was unaware of the picture they made, the small struggling captive and the towering, determined Viking. When Erik started to laugh and threw her over his shoulder, locking one arm over her kicking legs, she might have been disconcerted to know that a pair of thoughtful, watchful eyes followed them.

Thorolf watched them go, idly stroking his beard in contemplation. He could not recall when, if ever, he had heard his serious eldest son laugh so freely.

"Put me down, you lame-brained steroid abuser!" Lorelei shouted her demand while pummeling Erik's impervious back. With the amount of muscle and bone he had, he probably didn't feel a thing. It was definitely irritating.

She got her wish with an abruptness that almost knocked the wind out of her. Erik dumped her onto her back in a bed of grass and followed her to the ground before she could recover and roll away.

He pinned her with one leg over hers and one hand holding her wrists. She eyed him warily and decided she didn't like the serious look in his eyes one bit. Knowing him and his penchant for obedience, he'd probably decided that she really did deserve retribution for kicking him in front of the jarl.

So when he began to pull up her shirt, she assumed the worst. She also panicked and forgot everything she'd learned about self-defense, resorting to wild, undirected struggles that were quickly subdued.

He wrestled her flat and sprawled full-length over her, surprised at the strength his little slave had. She was no easy woman to overpower despite her slight stature. "Cease your struggles," he ordered, afraid he would hurt her.

Then he saw the fear and horror in her clear sea-colored eyes. Tears streaked her face, and the sobs that wracked her struck him like an unseen blow.

Freya, she thought he meant to force her.

"Cease," he repeated, more softly. "You have nothing to fear. Be still."

She stilled, but her miserable expression told him she expected brutal ravishment while she lay helpless. Despite himself, Erik smiled at her and teased, "I admit this grove has hidden many lovers. It is a pleasant and private place, for all it is close by to many dwellings." He stroked the curve of her lower lip with one finger. "I would enjoy a tryst with you amid the sweet grass and wildflowers. It is in truth a pleasant thought. But I stopped here for a different reason."

Her eyes silently invited him to continue.

"I would know if you are hurt." With that, he levered his weight to the side and leaned over her to protect her from any prying eyes that might chance by before baring her to his sight. "You will tell me if you feel pain."

"Of course I feel pain," she muttered. "You just squashed me. And I told you I don't want you touching me."

"That is unfortunate, since I will be touching you a great deal," he informed her. He suited actions to words, running his hands over her. "Do you hurt?"

She got it when one hand cupped her between her legs. Gently. The tangle of emotions that gesture stirred made the tears fall faster. Damn him, how could he be gentle and concerned in private, after the way he'd treated her in public?

And how could he have left her last night after what they'd shared?

Lorelei buried her face against his chest, ridiculously not wanting him to see her face while he touched her naked body as if that was more intimate.

He withdrew his hand and pulled her into his embrace. Strong arms wrapped around her and held her comfortingly close, and his chin rested against the top of her dark head. The husky timbre of his voice rumbled in his chest beneath her ear as he asked, "Is the hurt to your feelings once more?"

She nodded, not wanting to speak.

He sighed. "These feelings of yours are too easily damaged."

She sniffed. "I hate you."

"This I know. But it changes nothing."

"Obviously," she snapped. "And my feelings are connected to my body, so prepare to deal with them being hurt often."

He sighed again and sat up with her still in his arms. "I have no wish to see you suffer hurt of any kind. But since your body is undamaged, you will doubtless spend the night hours with hurt feelings as you will spend them in my bed."

"You don't have a confidence issue, do you?"

"I know not this issue you speak of. I do know that you belong to me."

He was so damn sure of her. Probably because the last time they'd argued she'd ended up abandoning the fight and coming her brains out instead.

And then he'd left when she needed him to hold her.

She wanted to hit him.

He tugged her chin up, forcing her to look at him. "You know I speak the truth," he insisted quietly. "Look at me and tell me you want me to take another to my bed."

She'd kill him. She'd kill both of them, him and whatever slut he cheated on her with. She knew it showed instantly on her face and she was helpless to hide it. They might not have any kind of conventional relationship, but dammit, they had a relationship. He was always going on about how she belonged to him. Well, it went both ways. He was *hers*.

Erik smiled at her. Then he kissed her.

Unfair, she thought. The kiss was as possessive as it was persuasive, devouring and...delicious. Unfair that he could override her pride, her self-respect and her self-control with a kiss. Unfair that his lips made hers soften and cling and eventually part for his invading tongue.

Unfair, maybe. But when he kissed her, she kissed him back and it turned torrid. Heat raced through her, and anger and hurt were channeled into desire. She tangled her fingers into his beard to keep his lips from moving away. She barely noticed his hands digging into her mass of hair to do the same.

He wasn't bent on any kind of a lesson. He wasn't laying down the law or giving orders. He was caught in the fire of need as thoroughly as she was, and there she found they were equals. She realized dimly that he was fighting it as fiercely in his own way as she was in hers.

Don't fight it, she wanted to say, and said it with her open mouth and hungry lips instead. *Don't fight me.*

She arched into him, demanding and inviting in the wordless, timeless language of lovers. His hands moved over her, taking what she offered. A taut nipple, tugged. A curved hip, squeezed. The fierce strength in his grip and the wild devouring heat in his kisses told her that his emotions were burning out of control at her response. That he wanted her. That her passion fired and fed his.

His lips broke away from hers and moved over her cheeks, eyes and forehead in a tender salute as his hands moved to her back, stroking the curve of her spine and bringing her closer.

Lorelei turned her cheek against his chest and curled into him, holding him as well as her bound wrists allowed. He was the most unbelievably inconsistent barbarian. If he was rough and uncaring, she could hate him until doomsday. Or Ragnarok, since that was the appropriate Viking equivalent. But he wasn't. He was gentle, passionate, and far from unemotional. She had the sure sense that he was caught up in the same relentless grip of feeling that made her his captive far more securely than a length of cord.

He was right, she admitted silently. She didn't want him to sleep with another woman. She didn't want to lose him, and she definitely didn't want to share.

Because in spite of everything, she'd fallen in love with him.

Lorelei let the realization sink in, accepting the truth as she accepted the hugs, kisses and caresses that were his way of showing her how he felt.

Love made her open her heart and soul and lay aside the unconscious barriers that had kept him out of her deepest awareness. The sure sense that always told her when something was right and what someone wanted reached out to Erik and embraced him. And everything in her opened to him in trusting acceptance.

Quiet certainty flooded her. This was right. *He* was right. The two of them together, right. He would fight it, but he wanted her too badly to let her go. And he cared too deeply to be the cause of her unhappiness. If he kept her a slave, it would cost him his heart's freedom. She felt danger ahead and knew it came from this time, this place. She couldn't stay. It wouldn't accept her, she was too different. But if he could bend, the future would open to him.

She shivered at the premonition. They hung between two possibilities. If she won his heart, he would release her and follow her to her world. And if she failed...darkness and danger grew until they overwhelmed her.

If she failed, she would die. His world would kill her.

Chapter Twelve

"Why so quiet?" The low question, breathed against her cheek, brought Lorelei abruptly back to present awareness. For a shaken minute, she simply regrouped mentally.

He thought she was nutty enough without hearing that she'd just seen two possible futures. That would really make him wonder about her, wouldn't it? Although she conceded that it might just make him think she was the world's greatest storyteller. Skald, that was the word. Funny, she wasn't much of a storyteller in her own world and she'd always wanted to be. At least one of her dreams was coming true.

Two dreams, if she counted falling in love. She'd always wanted to and never could understand why it didn't happen. She'd decided she didn't have it in her, and that her musical talents were a bonus of sorts to make up for whatever she lacked emotionally. It had seemed more and more bitterly ironic that what she could convey to a crowd through music, she couldn't feel herself.

"Lorelei? Woman, what are you thinking?"

She tipped her face up to his and regarded him soberly. "That you were right."

He raised one brow, plainly dubious.

She nodded, confirming that yes, she'd really said what he thought she just said. "You were right, Erik. It's different here. It's dangerous. I understand now why you were so concerned."

She shivered at the thought of just *how* dangerous it was. Quietly, she went on, "I'll obey you."

He didn't look convinced. But he did look slightly relieved. She realized then that he'd been waiting to see her reaction to the naked desire in his kiss. Wanting to be sure she truly did still want him, in spite of his macho act. Oh, she had no doubt that he would have hauled her off to bed if she hadn't responded. But he would have slept with her, the way he'd slept with her on the boat. He would have insisted that she sleep naked in his arms, but beyond that he wouldn't have touched her, and the knowledge warmed her further towards him.

He wanted her to want him.

Since she was feeling generous, she kissed him and then snuggled happily in his muscular embrace. "I promise, Erik. Word of honor. I didn't understand before," she assured him.

"And you wish me to believe that you will become compliant and obedient?" The doubt in his voice made her laugh, and she drew back to look up at him.

"Yep. You betcha. I'll be the best love slave you've ever had."

Instead of looking reassured, the plain disbelief grew. But he answered, "You are the only love slave I have had. It would take no great effort to be the best."

"Oh, come on," she retorted. "You expect me to believe that? A guy like you? You must haul women home by their hair by the busload."

He frowned. "By the what?"

"Often," she clarified, trying to be helpful. "And don't try to sidetrack me. You have other slaves."

"I do," he agreed. "But they do not sleep in my bed."

"Hm. What do they do?" Lorelei asked, really wondering.

"They care for the sheep and spin wool. Cook and serve the food. Clean. Feed the fire. Many things." While he answered her,

Erik redressed her and then frowned at the inadequate covering. "You need clothing."

"Yep," she agreed. Since she was being obedient and compliant, she didn't remind him that he was responsible for the fact that she needed clothing. Not gloating and saying "I told you so" had to count for some points, didn't it?

Of course it did, she assured herself, feeling smug.

He finished covering and straightening her to his satisfaction, then caught her face between his hands. His eyes were serious, probing hers deeply. "Woman, speak the truth. Have you accepted that you are mine, or do you wait for a better chance to run away?"

She started to answer, then stilled.

She shivered, suddenly deeply afraid and feeling a growing dark oppression. "Erik, I'll tell you the truth. I don't exactly agree with you about everything, but I do understand your reasons. Let's just say that I can't afford not to be reasonable."

He watched her face for some time in silence. Finally, he said, "You are still angry?"

She shook her head free of his grasp and laid it on his shoulder, not wanting to let him see the deep shadow of hurt in her eyes. The fight they'd been having before it got sidetracked by fear and lust had been important, and it still lay unresolved between them. She couldn't help being a product of her time any more than he could help being a product of his. And his lack of faith in her hurt. He let her hide her face, and after a moment, his hand cradled the back of her head in a comforting gesture.

"Erik, I don't really want to talk about it. Not now. You wouldn't understand. If you knew me better..." She trailed off with that thought.

He laughed softly and ran a possessive hand over her breast, teasing the nipple that budded at his touch with his thumb. "Woman, I know you better than any man."

The blunt sexual meaning was plain.

For some reason, it irked her. "Yeah, and you love that, don't you?" she grumbled.

"That no other has had you? That all this—" his hands moved over her with rough urgency, effectively making his point, "belongs to me?"

"You keep saying that."

"I say it because it is true."

Smug, sure, satisfied. That was her Viking. Lorelei sighed at the masculine arrogance. It was all the more galling because, dammit, it *was* true.

"Yes," Erik said, tightening his hold on her. "It pleases me more than I can say that no other has touched you. Would it please you to hear how your beauty delights me?" The husky warmth in his voice made a low throbbing build inside her in response to his sexual praise. "You are beautiful, and all your beauty belongs to me."

He caressed her breasts again, stroking them with open palms. Lorelei shivered at the touch. A languorous heat began building in her, and she felt her breasts swelling in his hands as if they were ripening for him, growing plump and ready.

She felt a low shudder go through him, and then he stood, sweeping her up in his embrace. "Woman, I want you. I want you now," Erik grated out.

The fierce need conveyed by his hands and his voice made the building heat spread, awakening a response. She clung to him, silent, pressing closer to him in wordless surrender.

He crushed her against his chest, demanding in a taut, low voice, "Have you forgotten your anger? Will you fight me?"

Too many questions she couldn't answer. Too many conflicts swirling around them. She'd fight him to hell and back before she'd let him break her, but she could give herself to him and give them both what they needed.

With sure insight, Lorelei knew it wasn't purely sexual, although the need had become a physical demand that neither of them could deny.

No, it was the almost desperate need to come together, to find closeness that drove them both.

With shaking hands, Lorelei touched his chest, tracing the contour of muscle with a mixture of wonder and aching desire. "Erik," she whispered, brushing her lips against the column of his throat. "How far is it to your place?"

For a moment, he stood as if turned to stone by her words. Then he was throwing her over his shoulder and moving in long, swift strides as he growled in reply, "Not far."

It wasn't far, but the ride seemed endless. It was oddly erotic, lying over his shoulder, his hands gripping her thighs and buttocks, her breasts pressing against his back. Lorelei closed her eyes and let him carry her, clinging to the knowledge that he needed her, needed the most primitive proof of his possession, needed her willing response.

She was his woman. She couldn't deny him.

Later, she would wonder what his other slaves, servants and neighbors thought of his determined rush through the village to his door and through it, to the small chamber at the end of the long hall. At the chamber door, he set her down, grabbed her bound wrists and dragged her through it, slamming it shut behind them and all but throwing her up against it. His knife slashed through the rope binding her legs, and then he was crowding up against her, demanding, "Spread."

She shivered, feeling almost frightened of the primitive emotions swirling through him. The hesitation made him raise her arms higher in a swift, jerky motion, lifting her breasts, now heaving with her rapid, shallow breathing. The knife slashed again, cutting the shirt from top to bottom and baring her body to his sight.

The fierce hunger in his eyes sent a thrill of feminine awareness through her. As if he'd touched her physically, her nipples budded for him. Exultation leaped in his eyes at the sight.

"Spread," Erik demanded again.

Shaking, Lorelei obeyed, moving her feet apart.

"Wider."

She complied, and the deep satisfaction in his eyes scorched her as he threw off his garments, his hot gaze never leaving her.

Then he stepped between her open thighs and lifted her, cupping her naked buttocks in powerful hands, crushing her between the door and his hard, demanding body.

It was so like the previous night that it brought back the memory of panic, of the realization that she could lose him. And now she knew she could lose everything if she failed to win him as fully as he'd won her. Knowing how much was at stake froze her in a kind of stage fright and she understood exactly what the phrase "performance anxiety" meant.

What if she couldn't? "Erik," she started, then swallowed convulsively.

"Shh." He gentled, moving against her persuasively. "Hush. Come to me, woman. Give yourself to me." The seductive words penetrated the haze of arousal and fear. His lips found hers and took them, licking, biting, now unspeakably soft, then so brutally fierce that she tasted blood.

"Give yourself to me," Erik repeated against her mouth. "Open for me. Open your mouth."

She did, shivering, as his tongue probed and claimed, thrusting between her lips as his hard penis moved against her softest, most vulnerable flesh.

"Open for me," he whispered, kissing her eyelids, her throat, her bared breasts.

A strangled cry escaped her as his lips tasted a pebbled nipple, drawing it into his mouth.

He seemed to take on a dreamlike aspect that rendered him all-powerful, undeniable. A pagan god, bent on subduing her, bending her to his will.

She shook in his hands and buried her face against him. It mattered too much. She was shattering with emotion and the blinding need for him. "I'm scared," she mumbled, the words muffled by his body.

"Sh," he crooned, soothing her with kisses, his hands sure and strong on her body. He lifted her higher, cradling her in his arms as he carried her to the bed and lowered her onto it, following her down and positioning himself at her unready opening.

"Erik—please—" Her voice sounded thin and strange to her ears.

"Hush." The low command made her tremble, but she obeyed. "Woman, open to me. Open for me." He moved against her, gentle but determined. "Look at me," he grated out, and her eyes opened, staring wildly into his.

"You belong to me." The statement caressed her like velvet and went through her like steel.

Yes. She was his, and she needed him. She shook with it. "Erik—"

He carefully propped himself on one arm, freeing a hand to lay it over her heart. "Your heart races like a frightened hare," he whispered. "Do you sense the snare of the hunter?"

His lips followed his hand, brushing over her hammering pulse.

Then he kneeled between her thighs, lifting her hips as his blue gaze burned into wide eyes turned the color of stormy seas. "Open for me, woman."

She shook her head helplessly, unable to obey, unable to move.

His hands pushed her thighs further apart and his body trapped them wide-spread for his ravishment. Then his mouth closed over her cleft and she cried out, shock waves racing through her.

"Sh. Shh, woman." He pressed intimate kisses along the length her mons, licked at her clitoris, and then he speared her with his tongue.

"Erik. Erik," Lorelei gasped, feeling fire shoot through her as he softened her, opening her with determined lips and fingers and sucking at her sensitive clit until liquid heat welled between her thighs and spilled for him.

"Open for me," he commanded again, and she did, straining to offer more of herself for him to take.

"Sweet," he whispered, moving his mouth over her and licking deep inside her again. Then he rose over her and came down to crush her into the bed, his jutting erection hard and hot between her thighs. His hard tip pressed deep into the cleft that welcomed him with slick readiness.

Still, he waited, prolonging the moment of his total possession of her. He gathered her close, wrapping his arms around her and hugging her against his chest. "Sweet Lorelei, give yourself to me," he urged, probing at her tight entry.

The meaning grew clear as he waited, not driving forward.

Hesitantly, she raised her hips, reaching for him and groaning softly as the tip pressed inside, making her ache for more. She arched up further and was rewarded by gaining more of his length, more of the sweet pressure she needed to feel filling her.

"Yes, woman. Sweet woman, my woman." The velvety words of praise were breathed against her cheeks and eyelids, his voice low and encouraging. "You want me inside you. You need me to come inside you. Tell me," Erik urged.

"I—need—"

"Not with words." He stole them from her with a deep, devouring kiss, leaving her to tell him the only way she could.

Wanting, aching, she wound her legs around his back and moved under him, straining to take more, to get closer. He settled deeper into her, riding inside easily and she cried out at the sensation.

Satisfied with her surrender, he claimed her with hard, sure strokes that soothed her need, driving into her welcoming softness again and again.

"Erik—"

"Hush, woman." The gentle admonition was breathed against her throat. He stilled for a moment, as if fighting the need to spill himself then and there. His hand found the bud between her legs once more, stroking it.

"Erik." She clung to him with almost desperate strength.

"Yes, woman. Take your pleasure from me," he encouraged, stroking the sensitive nub as he began to move inside her again.

The joint stimulation made the universe spin out of control. Shuddering, heaving under his crushing weight, Lorelei cried out again and again, not knowing her wild cries filled the room.

She knew only that she belonged to Erik, and he belonged to her. He drove into her with savage ferocity punctuated by each shattered cry wrenched from her throat, and then she was splintering, breaking, dissolving in a swelling liquid burst as Erik drove deep and planted his seed inside her welcoming female core.

Panting, he stayed still for long minutes, buried deeply inside her. Then he withdrew and rolled to his side, trapping her in his arms and legs to keep her pressed full against him.

"My woman." The husky claim, full of masculine pride, made her tremble.

"Yes," Lorelei agreed.

He stroked her with possessive hands, touching her nakedness with mingled satiation and greed.

"I will take you as I desire. And you will give yourself to me. You will not withhold yourself from me."

She trembled and burrowed into his embrace, feeling raw and shattered, not wanting to answer him.

When she remained silent, he brought her face up to meet his, smoothing back the midnight silk of her hair. "Say it, woman," he commanded.

"Erik." Her eyes dark with emotion, Lorelei touched his face, silently pleading with him to understand. "You don't know what you're asking."

"I understand that I have no need to ask," he stated. "You are mine by right. Say it."

She was his. She knew it, had recognized the truth of it and surrendered to it, but didn't know how to find the words to tell him.

"Say it."

"Erik." His name was a raw whisper. She closed her eyes and felt for answers. Words wouldn't be enough. How could she show him? How could she make him understand that he completed her? How to make him see that she completed him?

That they belonged together, were bound together by so much more than any law?

He took her silence for defiance. His hands gripped her with bruising force. "Say it."

Lorelei opened her eyes and met his steady gaze. "If I say I'm yours, is it enough?" She shook her head slightly. "You didn't believe me when I told you I'd behave. I don't think words are enough."

She took a deep breath and then put her heart and her future in his hands with her next words, reasoning that he held them both anyway. "I want to show you. I want to prove it to you so you never doubt me again."

A dark hunger erupted inside him at her words.

Freya, she drove him to madness and tempted him like no other. Would she truly surrender herself to him, prove herself his willing slave?

She belonged to him, and she had no choice in the matter. She had no right to withhold what was his. Yet he sensed that a part of her had always been kept back. He hungered for what she offered, what he had demanded of her. If she gave him all he asked or wanted, it would satisfy the hunger in his soul and lay to rest the fear that she was not in his power as utterly as he was in hers. For in truth, he had been hers from the first moment he laid eyes on her.

He reacted with the instinct to conquer, to take and hold what was his.

"You. Are. Mine."

The savage growl should have frightened her, or offended her modern woman sensibilities. Instead, her nipples hardened, her breath quickened, and heat pulsed between her legs.

Desire coursed through her. But she remained silent, waiting for him to take the lead. Waiting to see what he wanted of her. Feeling the erotic tease of uncertainty. He might ravish her right away. He might torture her with foreplay and delay her orgasm for hours. He might do...anything. Anything at all.

"You will admit it." The sexual heat and the ferocity in his eyes turned her bones to fire.

"I'm yours."

The breathy whisper came from her, unrecognizable to her ears as her own voice.

He came towards her, the need to possess written clearly on his face.

She shivered as she read the implacable determination in his eyes.

Her natural tendency to take charge told her to move forward to meet him, to touch him. Instinct told her to wait. With an effort of will she kept herself still. Submissive. His to do with as he pleased, although if he didn't touch her soon she was going to die. It didn't matter that she'd just had him inside her. She wanted him again.

Slowly, giving her time to move away or change her mind, his arms closed around her, surrounding her with protective strength. Then he fisted his hands in her hair and tugged her down in an unmistakable demand. Just in case she missed the point, he gave her an order. "I wish to feel my slave pleasure me with her mouth."

The submissive slave business was an unbelievable turn-on, Lorelei thought in a haze of blinding lust. She wanted to fill her mouth with him. She wanted to drive him as crazy as he drove her, to make him forget any other woman he'd ever touched, and most of all, to earn another sensual order to carry out.

Her lips brushed the tip of his penis and then opened to slide down the length of him, taking as much as she could into her mouth. He tasted like musky, salty, heated male. He was hard and thick and long. She wrapped her tongue around him, moving her mouth up and down him, sucking, licking, luxuriating in having him right where she wanted him.

Long before she'd had enough, he made a choked sound and pulled her head away. "Enough."

She looked up at him and licked her lips. It wasn't enough, but she didn't argue. She just waited.

"Lay back."

She obeyed. A tremor of anticipation wracked her from head to foot, but she didn't move, waiting for his next order.

"Spread your thighs."

Lorelei opened her legs as wide as she could stretch them— and with her flexible muscles, she could do the splits.

He leaned over her, looking down at her. Then he thrust one finger into her. He withdrew it, then thrust it in again.

She whimpered. He could torture her like this for hours. All night. It was killing her. But she managed to keep still.

"My slave is hot and wet for her master," he stated. He pulled his hand back and considered her for a moment. "Turn over. On your knees."

She did it, hopefully with some semblance of grace, but it was hard to say. Need made her clumsy and her bound hands didn't help. She closed her eyes as she felt Erik positioning himself behind her, felt the hard head of his cock resting against her slick, wet opening, and wanted him more than she could stand.

"Beg me," he said.

"Please!" The urgency in her voice was unmistakable.

"Call me master."

"Please, master." There was no shame in admitting it. He had mastered her, body, heart, mind, soul. With everything that she was, she belonged to him. Whatever had brought them together, she would never regret it. She had been born to be his, and he was hers. The more he owned of her, the more she owned of him. In surrendering everything, Lorelei suddenly realized, she had driven him to do the same. Neither of them was holding back anymore.

He thrust into her. She bit her lip to keep from moaning her pleasure. The feel of him inside her, so hard and hot and male, deeper inside her than he'd ever been before, made her want to move and make demands of her own.

His hands trailed along her sides and brushed the curve of her breasts, making her want more. As if responding to her silent plea, he cupped her breasts and thumbed her nipples.

Yes. She clenched around him, unable to prevent the reflex as her inner muscles tightened on his penis, drawing him even deeper inside.

He let out a low growl in response. Then he began to thrust in earnest, in, out, deeper, harder, taking her, giving himself, and finally pouring himself into her as they both surrendered to their mutual need, her rippling orgasm milking his cock until they were both utterly spent.

They collapsed together.

But there was still something left undone. Words that had to be said.

"I love you, Erik."

She felt him go still.

"Lorelei?" Her name was a question and a command all in one.

"Yes."

Silent, he held her and trailed his hands over her compliant form. "Yes? Yes, Erik, do you mean?"

"Yes, Erik."

"You will do as I say?"

She turned her head to look at him. "Yes. I said I'd obey you."

Dark, unreadable eyes burned into hers. "Whatever I command."

She quirked her mouth into a grin. "Don't command me not to want you."

He turned her, tugged her underneath him and lowered himself over her, trapping her. "And if I did?"

She slipped her legs around his waist, hugging him to her since her arms weren't free. "I think we both know that's a lost cause. Don't tease me, Erik."

"Teasing is not what I intend." And then he was hard and demanding and thrusting into her again.

Much, much later, Erik looked at his sleeping slave and wondered at the savagery she aroused in him.

He'd taken her repeatedly, wanting to subdue her. He had not been gentle, driven by his fierce need to conquer and possess her.

And she had taken him each time, welcoming him with soft cries and sweet heat, not complaining even though he knew she must be tiring. The last time, he had held her face between his hands and watched her eyes as he filled her. She should have ached from his demands, but still her eyes glowed with desire and she'd moved under him readily, needing him as fiercely as he needed her.

"*I love you,*" she'd said.

He touched her mouth, swollen and bruised from the savagery of his kisses. She sighed at his touch and Erik gathered her gently into the circle of his arms, needing to hold her close and keep her safe.

He cradled her against himself, stroking the silk of her skin and sending her into a deeper sleep. Small and trusting, she curled into him with a soft sound of pleasure.

It was unlike him to use a woman so roughly. He was no abuser of women, no rapist, no unskilled lover. Yet somehow she drove him to a level of wanting that had allowed him no gentleness and a ferocity of need that drove him to take her and take her long after he'd spent himself, until his pleasure came with no liquid release.

It was almost as if some deep, primitive part of himself needed to mate and mate without ceasing until he could be sure of impregnating her with his seed. As if he needed that total possession of her, that even her womb must belong to him, must swell with his seed.

At the thought, a fierce gladness welled up inside him.

He wanted to make her utterly, completely, undeniably his.

He wanted to know that his child nestled in the depths of her woman's body, shielded and nurtured by her.

Following his thoughts, he caressed her belly, laying his open palm against the slight swell. He had taken her so often that even now it was very likely that life quickened beneath his hand.

Cupping one breast with his other hand, he tested the soft weight in his palm. She was small, but round and womanly. Her breasts would nurture his babe readily.

He stroked the rosy nipple, thinking of a tiny mouth drawing on it.

And what status would their child hold? Freeborn or slave? There was a third answer to their dilemma. If he made her his wife, she would be free and yet bound to him and under his protection. She had vowed her love for him. If she loved him, she would stay. He could protect her. His woman and any children they were gifted with would be his to care for, and his sword and his strength would keep them from harm.

Lorelei stirred at the touch, beginning to wake. "Erik?"

He folded her closer, releasing her breast and brushing a tender kiss across her brow. "Sh. Sleep, my sweet."

She yawned, her eyes still closed. "I thought you wanted me..." she murmured with drowsy languor.

"I always want you," he whispered, kissing her mouth as softly as the brush of a butterfly's wings. "Sleep, now."

She gave a small smile at his words. "Always want you, too," she sighed.

He cuddled her as she slipped back into sleep, stroking the tangled silk of her hair, feeling a deep peace and content steal over him.

His woman, in his arms, where she belonged. She had given herself to him, admitted that she was his. That she loved him. He stroked her stomach again with gentle fingers, thinking of the future and what it might hold.

She was so proud, so defiant, his woman. Yet she had ceased to deny the bond between them. No matter how often he might anger her, he had no fear she would seek divorce. She had admitted that she was his woman in truth. And when any two of equal pride and strength came together, they were sure to drive each other to anger as easily as they drove each other to lust.

Marry her. Why not?

He considered the idea as he held her sleeping form.

She admitted she belonged to him. She had surrendered herself to him, again and again. That had been difficult for her, he knew. She had the pride of a Viking as surely as if Danish blood ran in her veins.

She would see that marriage benefited them both. And then there was the possibility that they had made a child between them already. The future status of their children must be secured. Even his fierce, proud slave could not deny that.

Slowly, his hand caressed her softly curved belly again.

Determined, Erik brushed another kiss across her sleeping face and settled the fur over her. He wondered if she had noticed that he had kept the lynx skin she preferred. He would make her a gift of it, he decided. Fine new silks, velvet and wool for gowns would please her, also. And jewels. His beautiful woman deserved a gift that would complement her rare loveliness. Emeralds to match her eyes, if any mere stone could.

Thinking of how he treasured her, how he would cherish her, he kissed her again and slept deeply, holding his woman close.

Chapter Thirteen

Lorelei woke in stages, feeling as if she lay wrapped in layers of clouds. Hazy, vague and not quite real. Tentatively, she stretched and extended a leg and discovered that some things were very real.

"Ouch."

The soft complaint escaped her as she became all too aware of sore, aching thighs. And breasts. And arms, and...she gasped and clapped a protective hand over her most abused, throbbing ache. Right between her thighs.

Then she realized her hands had been cut loose some time during the wild interlude. She guessed he'd been safe enough on that count. She was in no condition to run anywhere. Not that she would want to. She'd been exactly where she wanted to be and she had made her point with every screaming orgasm. Or maybe he'd made his point, there.

How dumb she'd been to fight a losing battle for so long, when all it took was unconditional surrender to win the war. Erik loved her. She knew it to the depths of her soul. He might never say the words, but he had shown her what she meant to him all through the night.

Although just now she felt every aching muscle she'd exerted waking up to complain about how thoroughly she'd overdone it. Well, that was his fault. If he hadn't been so insatiable and she hadn't been so turned on by that, she wouldn't be in this condition. Since it was his fault, she reasoned, she wanted him to soothe her. "Erik?"

Answer came in the form of a gentle hand stroking her hair back. She turned her face into it and kissed his palm. "Erik, I hurt," she whispered. "Make it stop."

"And how will I do that with you calling to me and kissing me?" Erik asked wryly.

"I don't know, but you're a resourceful kind of guy. You'll think of something," she assured him with blithe confidence. "I'm so sore," she added. "Were there two of you in this bed?"

He laughed at her outrageous question and scooped her up in his arms. "You give me the vigor of a hundred men," he teased.

"That many? Oh, dear." She sighed in mock dismay and snuggled into his embrace, looping her arms around his neck and rubbing her cheek against the smooth muscled wall of his chest.

"Or a thousand," he mused as her breasts brushed his chest and arms.

She giggled, a bright, happy sound. "I'll be happy to satisfy you a thousand times. But not just now. I hurt too much." She opened her eyes and smiled at him. "What time is it?" Lorelei asked.

"Night."

"No way. It's broad daylight," she protested.

"Night," he said again. "Remember you are in the North now. Be glad I'm feeling indulgent, you lazy slave. You've slept the day away."

"Mm," she agreed. "I was exhausted by a hundred men. Or was it a thousand?"

He hugged her so tightly that her ribs creaked. "Foolish woman. Praise my manly vigor any longer and you will find yourself on your back growing sorer still."

He carried her to a tub of water and lowered her into it.

"Nice," Lorelei commented, smiling up at him as the soothing heat closed around her.

"I knew you would wake soon," he answered, bending to kiss her mouth and each breast in turn. "I ordered water kept hot for you. My poor little slave, made to satisfy the lust of a hundred men. You must ache in truth."

"I do," she assured him. "And you forgot to kiss where it hurts most."

"I did?"

"You did."

He needed no urging to lift her naked form, water streaming over her breasts and belly in gleaming rivulets. "Where?" Erik asked, a light of devilment glinting in his eyes.

She touched a fingertip to the triangle of dark curls that grew between her legs. "Here."

"Ah." He kissed the soft curls. "Better?"

She shook her head slowly, feeling heat flooding her at the sensual game. "Lower."

His mouth moved down a fraction of an inch, obliging. Then he looked at her again. "Like that?"

"No." Her breathing quickened, Lorelei wet dry lips with her tongue and said huskily, "Lower."

He did, kissing her abused flesh with infinite tenderness, laving her raw ache with the soothing touch of his tongue.

A low groan escaped her. "Erik. Erik."

"Shh," he murmured, lowering her back into the water. "Stay in there, sweet woman, or I may slake my lust on you so thoroughly that you may never walk right again."

She giggled at the loving threat. "What a terrible fate."

She subsided into the tub, happy to let him care for her. He washed her with gentle, thorough hands. He lifted her out and dried her with soft cloths, then held her on his lap while he worked the tangles from her hair with a carved comb.

It was wonderful to be held like that, to be cared for like a child. She snuggled into him, hugging him close while he combed through the length of her hair in patient, slow strokes.

"Careful, woman," he murmured as her nipples rubbed against his chest, teased into hardness by the contact. "You will find yourself serving my lust once more, and I do not think you would enjoy it so much."

She grimaced at the truth of that statement. "Well, how long does it take to recover?" she demanded.

"Patience," he teased. He finished combing her hair and rocked with her in his arms for a moment. "Woman, you please me more than I can say."

"Good." Smug satisfaction sounded in her voice. "You please me, too."

"I know."

"How do you know?" She glared up at him in challenge, eyes narrowed.

Another rumbling laugh came from him at that question. "How do I know? Freya, I laid you five times this day and each time you were as ready and eager as the first. Think you I cannot tell that I please you?"

She considered that briefly. "Hmm. You have a point." She subsided, snuggling back into the curve of his neck. "Erik, I love you."

He nodded, resigned. "Now do I know you are my woman. You vow your anger to me one moment and your love the next."

"That isn't funny."

"Hush." His grasp tightened briefly and his lips moved over her temple. "Sweet, you had reason to be angry with me. It pleases me that you would lay aside your anger and come to my bed."

"Huh." Grumpily, she stared up at him. "You make it sound even worse than it is, somehow. You'll get me kicked out of every progressive women's movement from here to the twenty-first century," Lorelei complained.

"Cease your jesting. I wish to show you the rewards that await an obedient slave who pleases her master."

"Oh?" Questions showed in her eyes.

For an answer, Erik lifted her again and carried her to the bed, lowering her onto the silky fur. "Does this lynx skin please you?" he asked, brushing her nude body against the luxurious pelt.

"Yes," she whispered, looking at him with awakening desire.

"Then it pleases me to make a gift of it to you," he told her.

A small smile stole over her face. "Really? All that great sex and I get presents, too?"

He gave a mock sigh of regret. "Already she grows more greedy for my goods than for my manly form," he complained to the chamber. "Yes, you get many gifts this night. You pleased me, Lorelei," he stated with soft seriousness.

She grinned up at him.,"Tell me about my other presents."

"A fortune in fabrics." He scowled at her ferociously. "But I may think better of it and keep you as you are. I like my slave naked."

"I like it, too. But I understand winter is really cold," Lorelei suggested with hopefully slave-like meekness.

"I could warm you."

He made the offer generously, lowering his weight over her to sear her with his heat.

"Erik," she sighed, hugging him close. "You are so wonderfully warm."

"Yes," he agreed, weaving his hands into her hair. "But I suppose you must leave my chamber sometime or the tales of the helpless slave woman that I ravish while she screams in pain and terror will spread like plague and I will be forced to endure many curious visits from my neighbors."

She blinked at him. "Screams?"

"Woman, you screamed every time I took you. The servants thought you were dead when they brought the water in," he informed her. "The whole village is probably speaking in whispers, spreading rumors of my unusual manly proportions and vigor."

She felt her face burn with embarrassment. "Oh, no."

"Oh, yes," he assured her with solemn concern. "So I suppose you must have your new gowns, after all."

She had no answer to that, and Erik laughed out loud at her discomfit.

"Come, woman, thank me," he suggested, touching his mouth to hers.

She opened hers readily, inviting his sensual invasion. Well had she learned the day's lesson, he thought. Too well. He was nearly on the brink of taking her again, and it was too soon. He would pain her if he gave her no time to recover. Regretful, he broke the kiss and rolled off of her before his lusting body overrode his common sense.

"Come back here," Lorelei complained, reaching for him. "I thought we had a deal. If you make me hurt, you have to make it better. Presents aren't going to get you out of that one, Viking."

He turned to look at her, and frowned at evidence of the hurt she spoke of. "I may change my mind," he muttered. "If you leave my chamber looking like that, I will have Harold's sword at my throat no matter how well you are clothed."

She blinked. "Why? Did I turn ugly?"

"No. Never, sweet," he assured her, lifting her gently into his arms again and cradling her with infinite care. "But you bear the marks of my vigor." He touched her swollen lips and she grimaced.

"I think I see what you mean." She glanced down at her body, and groaned out loud at the darkening bruises that marked where he'd gripped her hips. Neither of them had noticed at the time. "Well, look at it this way, Erik," she suggested as she curled herself around him. "You'll have a fine reputation as a bad barbarian. This should put a good scare into the rest of your assorted slaves."

He refrained from telling her that he had already done that by dragging her into his chamber in the sight of all and then making her scream for hours. He had thought they were going to flee from him when he ordered water brought.

Deciding there was no need to mention that, Erik turned his attention to the woman in his arms. "How badly do you hurt?" he asked, touching her bruised hip.

"What? Oh." Lorelei looked at the bruise in question. "It's not as bad as it looks. I bruise really, really easily. I always have."

Still, he frowned looking at the evidence before him. He had been far too rough and there was no excuse. He would take more care with her in the future. "It will not happen again," he informed her, stroking her hip. "You need not fear my bed. I will be more careful."

"Erik, Erik," she sighed, shaking her head at him. "For a bright barbarian, you can really miss the point sometimes. You didn't hurt me, you big galoot. I bruise easily. It looks bad, but it doesn't hurt. It's here—" she took his hand and laid it over her dark triangle of curls–"that I need some TLC. I enjoyed it at the time, but now I think we overdid it."

"TLC?" He asked the question softly while he stroked her abused mound with a gentle hand, petting her.

"Sorry. An abbreviation, for tender loving care. Which I need. Love me, Erik."

He laughed at her request. "Do I do so, you will need more of this loving care immediately."

"What a great plan," Lorelei murmured.

"A foolish plan," he decided. "But you spoke truly. I will gladly soothe all your hurts."

"Good." She cuddled up to him, splaying her limbs to allow his gentle petting everywhere, and allowed herself to be soothed.

Oddly, his touch felt comforting, warm and nonsexual, even when he stroked her breasts and the soft triangle of hair between her legs. He kissed the tender, abraded flesh of her inner thighs, taking away the soreness with soft kisses and the softer caress of his beard. From head to toe, he made sweet amends to every abused part of her body until discomfort had faded and need thrummed in her.

Erik felt the change in her, from lassitude to awareness. Her quickened pulse throbbed beneath his hands and her breathing turned shallow. Reacting to her desire, he tasted the sweetness of her breast and heard her moan softly.

"So, woman," he whispered, reaching to trace the womanly cleft between her parted thighs again. "You grow ready for my taking so quickly?"

She shuddered in response, and he dipped into her, finding her ready. At the partial invasion of his fingertip, she gasped.

The blood raced in his veins, firing him once more to madness.

No longer caring if she ached, lost to all reason, needing the sweet warmth she gave to him, he rolled her onto her back once more and drove himself into her.

When she woke again, Lorelei knew she was alone even before she opened her eyes. As if the hours in Erik's arms had left her keenly attuned to his presence.

There was a nearly palpable sensation of absence and it carried with it a faint, uneasy foreboding that had her sitting up and glancing around the small chamber as if she expected a threat to appear from every shadow.

Ridiculous, of course. Still, the mood lingered, clung, and irritated like a badly made designer knockoff.

"You are overreacting," she announced fiercely, even as she hugged her knees to her chest in a protective posture. "What are you, codependent? You don't need Erik with you every single minute to feel secure."

Yes, she did, her uneasy emotions whispered. Erik would keep her safe.

"That's the stupidest thing you've ever said," Lorelei lectured herself in a stern tone.

Too bad it felt so true.

Without his protective bulk beside her, she felt terribly small and alone. And defenseless.

Well, she'd just have to adjust. Anyone would be nervous in a strange place, let alone a strange time. She just felt it more strongly since she was both. But she was adaptable. She'd get the hang of this place for as long as she was there.

More to the point, she'd get the hang of Erik and convince him to get them both out before disaster struck. He had the key, she was sure of it. Somehow, Dane's story and the legendary armbands that seemed to belong to Erik were connected, and they'd brought her across time to him.

"Of course," she murmured, snapping her fingers. The armbands. Two of them, one in each time. Forming a bridge, of sorts. Only she was here before the pagan ceremony that ended with one left behind and one carried into the future. So it hadn't happened yet, but the fact that she was there was proof that it would. Wasn't it?

She wavered between hope and uncertainty. Was there such a thing as fate? Destiny? Did her presence mean Erik would listen to her and get her home? Or were the fatalists wrong? According to the theorists, multiple probabilities existed in which every physical possibility played out.

Hardly a reassuring thought.

According to that, she could be in any possible past, and what happened would be anyone's guess.

With an effort, Lorelei mustered her bravado. She'd just have to think of Erik as a particularly difficult audience. No, more like a very important audition. Pivotal. It was imperative that she make a good impression. She could do that. She was good at it. She was very, very good at attuning herself to an audience and then shifting the audience to respond to her lead.

Meanwhile, she should pull herself together.

Towards that end, Lorelei hopped up and washed in the bowl of cool water undoubtedly left behind by her thoughtful Viking. Then she combed her long hair until it swept around her waist in a tidy, almost-tame fall.

Clothes were a problem. She considered various possibilities, and finally decided to find something of Erik's to wear. His breech-like pants were laughable on her, but with the remnants of her cords, she made a sort of belt and managed to keep them from falling off her hips. She tried one of his vests, but the size made that impossible; she would have been more modestly covered without it, since the gaping armholes and plunging vee displayed everything.

A shirt seemed the best solution, so she donned one.

She peered doubtfully at the result. It would have looked better by itself, she decided. But she didn't like the idea of running around bare underneath, for some reason.

Too vulnerable.

"Well," she murmured under her breath, "ready or not, here I come." Reminding herself that she was Lorelei Michaels, lead Siren, rock legend and so loaded she needed a private financial advisor, she straightened her shoulders and drew herself up to her full height. She had faced hostile audiences and played to crowds of thousands. She could face a few Viking-age villagers. Even if they had heard her screaming every time she came in Erik's talented hands. She nearly groaned at the thought and mentally damned him. Then she relented and grinned. No, she didn't regret his talents. And as for the lack of privacy, well, these people must be used to it. What was the oriental saying? Nudity was often seen, but never noticed? Well, maybe her vocal excesses would go unmentioned.

She could hope.

She drew a deep breath, threw open the door before her bravado evaporated and strode out into the hall as if she were strutting onto a stage.

Her hopes were dashed as the women cooking over the fire stared at her with mingled horror, pity and fascination.

Erik, she vowed inwardly, I am going to kill you.

Outwardly, she feigned confident unconcern and strolled towards them with a friendly smile. "Whatever that is cooking, it smells divine. Can I have some? I'm starved."

One woman let out a cry. "Do you hear? He starves her, also!"

Obviously, she was going to have to help herself. Lorelei searched for something to eat out of, found a wooden bowl and ladled the contents of the pot into it. Not seeing any spoons, she tipped it and drank the broth, pausing to chew vegetables and chunks of whatever kind of meat it was. Venison, maybe.

She finished and set the bowl down to see both women still staring at her.

"Poor child," whispered the second woman.

Sympathy shone in both pairs of eyes.

For some reason, it irritated her. And she wasn't sure which insinuation bothered her more, that they thought Erik was a monster, or that they considered her helpless in his power.

"I'm not a child," she snapped.

Although compared to their height, she probably did look younger than she was. And the oversized clothing didn't exactly give her an air of competent authority.

The women looked even more pitying. "Not any longer," the first one said.

Lorelei looked from one to the other and felt an overpowering desire to pound her head against the wooden table. Instead, she opted for a dignified retreat. She'd go for a short walk. Clear the cobwebs. Calm down. Without another word, she headed outside and into fresh air and freedom.

Once outside, she felt her good humor return. It was hard to hold onto a rotten mood when the sun never stopped shining. There was something not only cheery but positively invigorating about the extended daylight. Earthy scents like sun warmed grass, sweet blossoms and the salty tang of sea air assailed her senses, and everywhere she looked, she saw riotous color. The blue sky was bluer, the green grass and trees greener; everything was more vivid here. There was the sharp scent of wood smoke from cooking fires, and the mingled odors that went along with the presence of livestock.

Lorelei headed across a field, frowning in concentration. What had Erik told her, that he had sheep? Yes, he had. And as if her thoughts had conjured both, she saw him ahead with a group of men and the woolly sheep scattered like cotton balls on the green landscape.

She knew the moment he became aware of her. His head turned towards her, and he extended an arm in invitation.

"You don't have to ask me twice," she decided. On impulse, she raced towards him and launched herself into his arms on a flying leap, trusting him to catch her.

He did, grunting at the impact. He tried to frown at her, but she saw the smile lurking underneath. She beamed at him, radiant with happiness. "Hi."

"Your greeting lacks—"

"Respect and caution, right? I know the drill. Aren't you happy to see me?" Lorelei leaned closer and gave him a smacking kiss on the mouth. "I'm happy to see you. I missed you."

"Woman, I left you to sleep." Now he did frown.

"I did sleep," she informed him. "Honest."

Then she turned her head to include the two men standing by Erik in her smile. "Hi. I'm Lorelei." Beyond them, she suddenly saw something that transfixed and utterly distracted her. "Hey! Horses! Erik, you didn't tell me you had horses."

On the point of delivering a lecture on the importance of staying where he put her and thinking before she acted and above all, never interrupting him, Erik paused and looked at the picture she made. She was staring at his horses in much the way a small child gazed at a forbidden sweet. Her lips were parted as if in eagerness and awe.

In his mind, he replayed the moment he had seen her coming across the field. He had been unable to resist opening his arms to her. And the sight of her running to him, her long hair flying behind her like a banner, had started a warmth inside that grew and spread and weakened him so that he could not find it in himself to say anything that might take away her pleasure in the day.

Instead of lecturing her, he asked, "Would you like to ride with me?"

His reward was a look of awed gratitude and shining delight that turned her eyes the luminous color of very fine jade. "Oh, Erik. Could I?"

In answer he shifted his hold on her, tossing her up in the air and catching her against his chest. He grinned at Thorvald and Raynor and failed to notice their expressions of shock at his unprecedented good humor. "We will speak later at my father's."

With that, he turned and strode away with the girl in his arms. He let out a shrill whistle and a white stallion neighed in response. It came to the pair and waited while they mounted. In a flurry of galloping hooves, man, woman and horse wheeled about and shot into the distance like an arrow released from a bow.

The two men stood gaping after them for some moments. At long last, two pairs of stunned eyes met.

"Was that Erik Thorolfsson? Erik the Unsmiling? Black Erik?" Thorvald inquired. The last name referred to temper, not hair color. Erik was a cold, controlled man, some might even say grim, but he had a temper that even the Danes who were ever ready to fight took care not to provoke.

"It was," Raynor answered.

"He allowed a slave to be so familiar? To interrupt talk of business? And he leaves to indulge her whims?"

"It would appear so."

The two men stared after the vanished company in silence, stroking their beards in contemplation. The whole settlement had heard of the slave Erik had found in Hedeby and nearly fought over instead of buying. The returning traders had told a variety of tales. That she was mad. That she was a skald of extraordinary skill. That the two had fought the entire way home. And those who had not seen him drag her, half-dressed and kicking through the village to his home had heard that he used her so brutally that she was sure to die before the winter, indeed that she had already tried to take her own life to escape his lust.

Now here she was, behaving as if she could not bear to be without him for a moment, and gazing at him as if he had all of Odin's wit and Thor's strength besides.

"It would seem," Raynor mused at last, "that Harold has not all the woman-luck in that family."

Oblivious to the rest of the world, Lorelei was laughing in delight as the wind whipped her hair back. Her head lay on Erik's shoulder and his arms held her in a secure grip. She rested in his lap with absolute confidence that he wouldn't let her fall. When he finally slowed the horse and stopped, jumping down with her, she smiled her pleasure into his eyes and wondered how she had ever thought that shade of blue icy.

"Thank you. That was wonderful."

Her voice was so enthusiastic that he gave her a long look. "Am I to take second place in your affections to my horse now?"

"Never," Lorelei vowed. She wound her arms around his neck and dropped her cheek against his chest.

"Never? That is a long time."

"I think it's safe to say that your horse will never be able to compare with you."

The teasing note in her voice pleased him. Everything about her pleased him. "And certainly my horse cannot compare to you. You are by far more pleasant to ride." He tumbled her to the ground and kissed her, finding his way beneath the cumbersome shirt easily with questing hands.

"Mm," she sighed, melting under him. "Erik."

He smiled at the response and rolled to lay with his arms around her, looking into her eyes.

"What are you doing?"

"Looking at you. I may never tire of the view." He stroked her hair and smiled at her. Her beauty struck him anew and nearly stole his breath. She would only grow more beautiful when she was breeding. Perhaps she was even now. At the thought he shifted their positions so that he lay on the damp grass and she lay atop him. If so, he would guard with care the fragile new life. He would see to it that she took no risks, took no more wild dives into cold seas or pounding gallops over fields. Which made him realize that the breakneck pace he'd ridden at may have been a foolish risk.

"Erik, you're frowning."

"This ride may not have been wise."

"Why? Are you worried about bandits or whatever? I thought you had your sword with you."

"I always have my sword with me. And we are quite safe. The feast begins today to welcome us back, so every man in the settlement is nearby."

And every one of them lusting and eager for a glimpse of his prize. Erik's scowl darkened at the thought.

"Stop that." Lorelei smoothed away his frown lines with her hands and dropped kisses all over his face. "We're supposed to be having fun, here. Bonding."

"Bonding?"

"Yeah." She snuggled closer to him and let her fingers drift down to the inviting expanse of tanned, muscled chest his leather vest exposed.

"You have not had enough of that?"

Catching his meaning along with the doubt in his voice, Lorelei laughed out loud. "That's not what I meant. I'm talking about bonding. Do you realize that outside of bed, we've hardly done anything but fight? We need some quality time. We need to do things together that we both enjoy. Companionship."

He grunted, a noncommittal sound.

"Come on. You enjoyed the ride, right?"

"I did until I thought of the consequences. I should have been more careful with you. You might have fallen."

She let out a long, dramatic groan. "There you go again. I bet you're lots of fun at parties. Erik, you *were* careful. You know your horse, the ground and your own strength. You wouldn't have let me fall."

"We will still ride back slowly."

She gave a despairing sigh and fell silent.

He supposed she would not be pleased to know that he meant to leave her safe at his home instead of allowing her to bond with him at his father's, either.

Chapter Fourteen

She wasn't.

He broke the news to her after they returned from the ride, when they were in the inner chamber, where presumably the sound of her shouts would just be shrugged off as normal.

"You can't be serious," she protested. "I'm the entertainment, and you're not taking me to the big party?"

Erik frowned at her and it was easy to see where his mind was going. Lorelei sighed in exasperation. "Not that kind of entertainment. Singing."

He shook his head. "You have not sung for me, yet you sing for my brother and now you would sing for all the settlement."

Lorelei opened her mouth, then closed it again. Songs were important to these people, she'd picked up on that. And no wonder. Their history was in their oral tradition. To be remembered in song was to attain immortality. She was a singer, a skald in their words. She was Erik's slave by their laws, his woman by the law of her heart. And she had never sung for him. Not once had she given him the gift of her talent.

"I'm sorry. I should have sung for you."

He reached out to brush the long fall of her hair back over her shoulder. "You owe me no apologies. It is your gift to give as you choose."

"I should have thought of it." She leaned into him, simply for the joy of contact. "I just didn't. We were so busy fighting, and then, um, doing other things. I forgot."

Erik's hands twined lazily in her hair. It created a gentle tugging sensation along her scalp, almost like a massage and it made her sigh in pleasure. The simplest touch between them felt so good. But not good enough to make her drop the argument. "You should take me with you."

"You should stay here where you are safe."

He might have a point, there. But then, how safe would she be if they were separated? Anything could happen. She didn't like that idea at all. But before she could come up with a persuasive point, he continued.

"There is a man who bears a grudge against my family. All know that you are mine, that I took you at sword point because for a moment I stepped outside the law. Did I do so once for you, I may do so again. He may use you to have me declared outlaw. He could touch you, knowing I do not permit it, to drive me to retaliate unlawfully. Until you are my wife, he may think to use you against me."

Wife. The word completely derailed Lorelei. "Wife? Excuse me?" She gripped Erik's vest in both hands and stared up at him. "Did you propose to me and I missed it?"

He frowned down at her. "What is this propose? I give you my armband, which should please you since you have been fixated upon it from the beginning. We drink from one cup. And then are you my wife."

"Like in the story." She said it without thinking. And then she remembered.

She had put the armband on in her time while she thought about the story Dane had told her. She'd thought about the two lovers who had each other while she had nobody. She'd wanted what they had. *Really* wanted it. And she had sort of boiled over inside, the way her emotions boiled over into singing, only she hadn't been performing. She'd done something else with that internal force. She'd made a wish.

Be careful what you wish for.

That wish had been the key, or rather, the mental force she exerted had been the key. Because she was psychic. Clairvoyant was the proper term. And there was probably a word for her ability to manipulate music to broadcast emotion, too.

It was a just part of her, something she didn't think about very much. Something she usually avoided thinking about, since it wasn't logical or predictable. It just was. Sometimes she knew things, felt things. And she'd learned early never to go against the things she knew, no matter how irrational they seemed, because they were always right. Not only had she come to depend on that part of herself, those around her had, too. The rest of the band looked to her to make decisions about tour dates and locations, timing of album releases, and all sorts of business details.

The dream had said she was the key, and like a key turning in a lock, she understood. She had wished—willed—to find what the lovers in the story had, and the armbands, one in each time, had activated and brought her across the years in a heartbeat.

If she married Erik and put the armband on again, she could activate them. And he might not want to go home with her. Or, willing or not, he might not be free to go.

Lorelei thought about the number of people who worked on his farm. They were more than his employees. They depended on him in a more feudal sort of relationship. And presumably they in turn had families depending on them. She hadn't missed the importance of a successful trading voyage to this isolated community, or that he was a natural leader. If he left, it would leave a big gap.

Complication on complication. Now she knew how to get home. Erik was willing to give her the means to do it. And that meant either leaving him, which now seemed unthinkable, or asking him to abandon his responsibilities. A thing he could never do. She hadn't known him long, but she knew how deep his sense of honor and duty went.

"I tell you I plan to make you my wife. This should please you. But whenever do you behave as I expect?" Erik was frowning at her, but behind the expression on his face, behind the words, was hurt. She knew it. She felt it.

"Erik—"

"Ah. I looked to find the two of you ready for the celebration, and here you hide, fighting instead." Harold stood in the doorway to Erik's private room, smiling at them both in obvious good humor. "Or it may be that you have grown so heated from arguing that you must throw me out and close the door to cool down in that bed. The hour is likely to grow very late do you not come with me now instead. There will be no food or drink left by the time you two think to rise and join us. And I would miss my favorite skald singing to me while I grow drunk. It is your turn to sing while I drink," he pointed out to Lorelei.

Well. If she was going to tell a wild story, she might as well do it while she had both of them for an audience. "Harold. Glad to see you. Come in and shut the door."

That surprised both men. But Harold did come in and shut the door behind him. Undoubtedly because he knew his presence was irritating his big brother.

She let go of Erik and stepped back so she could look at both of them while she talked. "I need to tell you a story. And then, Erik, you have to decide if you really want to marry me. Because you might change your mind."

Harold shouted and clapped his brother on the back so hard she was surprised the blow didn't knock him over. "By

Thor, you do have the wit to take this prize to wife! I nearly despaired of you."

"Um, not so fast on the congratulations," Lorelei sighed. "Here's the story. Once upon a time, a Viking and a Valkyrie fell in love. Only maybe she wasn't really a warrior, maybe she just had a little bit of a temper and was used to getting her way so they fought a lot. You know how these things get blown out of proportion. Anyway, they fell in love. They married. And when he gave her his armband and she put it on, they disappeared. She took him with her to Valhalla, the story goes. Or maybe she took him someplace else. Like into the future with her, where she came from."

She paused and took a breath, hoping it wasn't wasted. Hoping they believed her, or at least were willing to consider the possibility. "My friend Dane, who must be Harold's great-great-great-something grandson, had the armband because when they disappeared, hers fell off. He told me the story and gave it to me to wear. And when I put it on, I made a wish. I wished for love, like the people in the story. And I fell out of my time and landed in Heady-something, right in front of Erik. Who was wearing both of the armbands, only now they're new. The one in my time was old. And I put it on there, but I didn't have it when I got here. So it must still be there. In the future. Making a bridge. Because I don't belong here and I'm supposed to go back."

They were both staring at her now.

"I know. You don't have to tell me how ridiculous it sounds. I don't believe it either. Except I have to, because here I am, and here you are—" She waved at Erik, "And there are the armbands. And now you want to give me one and marry me. We're the people in the story. So you can't marry me, because you'd be abandoning all your responsibilities and you'd never forgive me for that," she finished miserably.

"Do you fail to take this woman as your wife, I will never forgive you," Harold said. All humor was gone from his face. "Never have I seen my dutiful older brother forget his responsibilities even for a moment. Until you set eyes on Lorelei, and drew your sword and for the first time in your life, took something you wanted for yourself."

He stood straighter and held Erik's gaze with piercing determination. "Are you not forever telling me I must learn my duty? That if I exerted myself to lead, I would do well? Well, then. Marry your woman and go with her. Travel upon the sea of time. Were I the one given the opportunity, I would take that voyage. And from childhood have you dreamed of great voyages even more than I."

He turned his head and smiled at Lorelei then. "But there is a price. If I am to be the dutiful son and marry Gudred and have these offspring to carry the armband down the years to you, you will make a song for me. The name of Harold Thorrolfson will live in memory. Is it a bargain?"

She grinned at him. "Yes."

They shook hands.

Erik shook his head at both of them. "My brother and my beloved have both lost their wits."

"Beloved?" Lorelei beamed at him. "You said it. I didn't think you'd ever say it. I thought we'd spend the next fifty years fighting and making up and you'd never actually say you loved me."

Erik reached out to take her by the shoulders and draw her against his hard chest. "Harold, you would do well to lead. All would follow you. But you think there is truth in this tale? Why?"

Great, she fumed. Ask the man. Not her, the woman who knew, because she'd been there and done that.

"Her clothing," Harold answered promptly. "Have you examined the garments she wore? Have you ever seen the like? For years you have traded with craftsmen and weavers throughout the world. You know well what fabrics are made and where. Look at them and tell me who has the skill to make such stockings as she wore?"

Her pantyhose? She wanted to groan in disbelief. She could tell them about world history, world events, technology, engineering. Okay, maybe engineering wasn't her strong point, but still, she would have thought those things would be of interest. And a pair of pantyhose was the thing that convinced them. Unbelievable.

Erik set her aside and the two men pulled out and examined her now-destroyed dress and her perfectly undamaged nylons like archeologists studying an ancient find.

"I have never seen the like," Erik said at last.

He was silent for a long moment. Then he asked Harold, "You will curb your wildness? You will abide by the law, uphold it, lead well?"

"I will. In truth, I missed Gudred this summer and she will not have me to husband do I not settle down." He looked crestfallen and Lorelei wanted to laugh, but managed not to. Big bad Viking, tamed by a woman.

"You said you believe you are meant to go back." Erik addressed her now. "You would leave me?"

"I don't want to," she answered quickly. And oh, God, she didn't. The thought of being without him again after knowing what it was like to have him...she would miss him for the rest of her life. "But Erik, I don't think I can stay here even if I wanted to. I think I did what I came here to do and I'm supposed to go back. If I don't, I don't think the story has a happy ending. I think I'd die here, in your time."

He looked fierce. "Die how? Have I not vowed to protect you?"

"You can't protect me from everything." She slid a sideways look at Harold, figured the entire settlement knew exactly what their relationship entailed anyway, and went on, "What if I'm pregnant already? There aren't any hospitals. Women die in childbirth here, or they get an infection and die after the birth. Most pregnancies don't have complications, but a pretty good percentage do. In the future, there are hospitals and surgeons and antibiotics and oxygen to save women and babies when things go wrong."

The possibility was something she hadn't exactly let herself dwell on. She'd never given up hope on finding a way back home. And if that meant she returned pregnant and ended up raising a child as a single mother, well, it wasn't her preference but she had the money to do it, even if she had to quit working for a while. Most women weren't in that position, but since she was, she'd made the inner choice to let the fates decide and not worry about the lack of birth control in the Viking age. If it happened, it happened. Although the more time she spent with Erik, the odds of it happening were going to keep increasing.

Erik gave her a long, considering look.

"You believe you will be returned to your time." He didn't wait for her to answer. He continued, "My child will not grow up fatherless. You will not live out your days without me at your side. We marry, and if the gods will it, you return to your home and I go with you."

Then he turned to Harold. "My brother, I will leave my property to you."

Harold nodded, accepting the responsibility. Lorelei thought he'd wear it well.

"Now, woman of the future. You came with what you were wearing. Therefore do we wear what we wish to take with us, it should travel as we do."

That made sense. The armband, Lorelei decided, was an anomaly all the way around. Everything else she'd been wearing had come along for the trip. "It should," she agreed.

While she watched, he gathered up a pack and filled it with everything he'd given her along with jewels, coins, the kind of things her practical Viking figured would translate easily into wealth in her time. That would matter to him, she realized. His pride would never allow him to live on her money. He would bring what he needed to provide for his family and begin a new life, and she didn't doubt for a minute that he'd be busy reinventing himself and building a new fortune as soon as they arrived. His ever-present sword in hand.

Lorelei fought a grin as she imagined Erik versus the modern day business world. No question, Erik would win. And it was going to be fun to watch.

Still, he was giving up a lot. His life. His family. Everything familiar.

"Erik, are you sure about this?" she asked. "You don't have to do this."

He smiled at her, and she saw it in his face. The spirit of adventure. The joy in his expression, as if a great weight had been lifted from him. "I had a dream. In it, I took you far from this place, far from the threat of punishment from breaking our laws. In this place, we could be free together and I could keep you safe. I dreamed of sailing away with you. Is this not like my dream?"

He came closer to her and touched her face. "Taking you for my wife is the only way to marry my duty and my heart. I cannot keep you a slave. I cannot leave you alone and unprotected to make your own way. You must be my wife, therefore. And if your tales are true, when I make you my wife we will journey away together as I wished to do. Although your winning personality will remain unchanged and doubtless we will fight as often in your time as we do now."

The prospect didn't seem to bother him. In fact, given the intensity of makeup sex, she was pretty sure he was looking forward to it.

"Okay, then. How do we do this? Here? At the party?"

"At the celebration," Harold suggested. "I wish to hear you sing again before you go. Sing the ballad of the Celt Bobby McGee."

So she did. She sang for a crowd of Vikings while they ate and drank and laughed and clapped. And then Erik pulled her onto his lap and held her securely while he drank from his cup, then passed it to her to drink from. She took a careful swallow, since she recognized it as the same stuff she'd been drinking with Harold. Some kind of moonshine, probably. Whatever it was, she had a healthy respect for its alcohol content.

He took one armband off and slid it up her arm.

Her husband. Her love. For all time.

Lorelei took a deep breath. And thought, *there's no place like home.*

They were back in the Emerald City, not Kansas. She could hear traffic and rain falling and she recognized the bedroom they were standing in. It was her room, in the house on Queen Anne Hill in Seattle that she shared with the band, and there was somebody sleeping in her bed. She felt mildly indignant about that, until he turned in his sleep and threw off the covers and she recognized him.

Beside her, Erik drew his sword.

"Friend," she told him quickly, trying not to laugh. "That's Dane. My friend. The one I confused with Harold. They could be twins, except for the beard."

Dane had probably panicked when she vanished and he found his armband laying there with no Lorelei in sight. But since he'd sent her time-traveling without any warning, she didn't feel too badly for him. And she wanted that bed. She hadn't forgotten about the sickening sensation that had made her pass out in Erik's arms after the first trip through time. She wanted to be laying on something nice and soft when it caught up with her.

She made for the bed and prodded at the muscled arm that hung down the side. "Move it. You're hogging the bed, the pillows, and all the covers."

He rolled over without waking up, and Lorelei sprawled gratefully on the open space he'd made. "Ahhh. A real bed. Heaven." She laid her head on a pillow and closed her eyes. "Erik, you'd better join me. Remember I was sick when you found me? Time travel causes the worst jetlag you can imagine. If you pass out, it should be where you can't hit your head on anything hard."

It was an effort to speak now, she realized. Everything was whirling around her. Oh, yes, and the headache was hitting her. She'd forgotten the headache.

She felt Erik's weight settle beside her, felt his arms pulling her against his chest, tucking her securely into his body.

She imagined Dane's face when he woke up and saw them and wanted to giggle. He must have the armband, she thought fuzzily, since they would have been dumped in its vicinity. The pair were reunited. And dangerous. *Have to throw them into the Sound or something*, she thought. And then she didn't think anything for a long time.

It was the noise that woke her up.

She groaned and tried to pull a pillow over her head, but something was weighing it down. Lorelei opened her eyes and blinked hard, trying to bring the world into focus.

Ah. Dane and Erik had met. She'd better interrupt them.

"Dane. Stop trying to kill my husband. And find somebody to get some coffee up here. Lots of coffee. I want Starbucks. I want chocolate covered coffee beans." Just the thought of coffee made her mouth water.

"Husband?" Dane stared at her, shock personified. "Where'd you find him, a biker bar for creative anachronism?"

Lorelei giggled. "No. He's a Viking. Your great-great-something or other. The one who had the armbands originally."

Speaking of which... She sat up in alarm. "You're not wearing the one you gave me, are you? Take it off! We have to get rid of them!"

Dane eyed her and sniggered. "Nice outfit, babe."

She looked down at Erik's shirt, pants, her makeshift belt, and shrugged. "I was a little fashion-challenged on the trip. But I mean it about the armbands, Dane. Where's yours?"

"On the table. There." He gestured towards a small table that stood under the window. Lorelei saw the glint of gold and silver from across the room.

"Oh, good, you don't have it on. Do me a favor and don't ever wear it. In fact, you can take the pair of them for a little sail on Iduna and dump them into the ocean."

Iduna, lover in Old Norse, was the name of Dane's sailboat. He'd left it moored in Seattle, since that was the last stop on the Legends concert tour. And what a perfect way to get rid of a Viking-age problem, Lorelei decided.

Erik made a low sound in his throat, and she realized he'd only understood one word in the conversation. Lover. The rest had been in English. She giggled and turned to kiss him. "We're talking about his sailboat. I told him to take the pair of armbands out to sea and dump them where nobody else can find them." She tangled her fingers in his beard and wished they were alone, free to take the kiss further. But then again, they had a few problems to solve first.

"In fact, Dane, maybe you should take us both out for a sail for a little while. It might be a good idea to keep Erik out of sight while he learns English and we get some papers for him. He'll need an identity package. And we have to get married again so it's legal here."

"Right. Because I have nothing better to do than be your errand boy." He rolled his eyes at her, but his relief at seeing her safe and sound was palpable.

"Hey, you sent me into the past. You created this time-travel mess, you can help fix it."

Dane looked at the two of them, indicating with a wave of his hand the way Erik's body curved protectively around hers, the way her fingers curled into his beard. "I don't think you came out of it too badly. Didn't I tell you you'd find the right guy? I think you should be thanking me."

"Thank you. Now let's sink those damn things in the bottom of the ocean before they cause any more trouble."

"Good plan." Dane scooted to the far side of the bed, stood, and picked up his boots. He'd fallen asleep fully dressed otherwise. "By the way, Morris hushed up your vanishing act and I talked him out of telling the authorities. I had a feeling about you and the armband's history. It seemed to make more sense than somebody kidnapping you when the security monitors didn't show anybody entering or leaving. You just vanished into thin air. You're a witchy woman. If anybody could take a trip through time, it'd be you. I figured if I was right you'd turn up pretty soon and wouldn't want any complications. The official explanation is your gall bladder. You were suddenly sick and had to have emergency surgery, concert cancelled."

"Oh, smart." Lorelei smiled with delight. "Good cover. And another good reason for us all to lay low for a little while. I can be recovering."

"I think you're right. I'll get everything set up. You two hide out here until I get back." Dane hesitated, then came close and offered his hand to Erik. Then he leaned down to brush a kiss on Lorelei's cheek. "I'm happy for you, babe. And so damn relieved. I saw that armband laying there, and I was afraid you were in trouble. If anything had happened to you, it would have been my fault. I shouldn't have given it to you."

"Yes, you should have. Everything happened just the way it should. Don't be sorry, Dane, because I'm not."

He looked from her to the big Viking beside her. "No, I guess you're not." He smiled at Erik. "You're a lucky man. You take care of her."

The words might not have translated, but it seemed the meaning did because Erik nodded at Dane. Probably a guy thing, Lorelei mused. As Dane left, she called after him, 'Don't forget about the coffee!"

"What is this coffee?" Erik asked her.

"Ah. An item of trade. You'll like it." She smiled at him, and then used her fingers threaded through his beard to tug him down for another kiss, this time a more thorough and leisurely one. They had all the time in the world now.

One Year Later...

"Happy anniversary."

Lorelei smiled at the sound of her husband's husky voice against her ear. She stretched, feeling the hard, muscled length of his body against hers, the heat of him warming her back. Silk sheets slid under her bare skin. And the unmistakably hard length of his erection was pressed against her butt. "Happy anniversary to you, too. What a nice way to wake up. And is that a sword between your legs, or are you happy to see me?"

"I am very happy to see you."

The sensual intent in Erik's voice made her smile wider. "Ohh, good."

He slid one hand along her side, down her thigh, then between her legs. She shifted obligingly to allow him better access and sighed her delight as he cupped the pad of her mons, then found and stroked her clitoris. "I wonder if my wife would like to play a game this morning?"

A happy giggle escaped her. "What kind of game did you have in mind?"

"The Viking and his love slave."

"Sounds fun. What are the rules?"

"One rule. You belong to me. And I take you." As he spoke, he thrust two fingers into her. Hard.

Liquid heat drenched the fingers invading her and spread through her body, bringing with it a lassitude that turned her bones weak and made her melt into him. Life in the twenty-first century hadn't changed him. He might have cut his hair, shaved off his beard and changed the way he dressed, but he still did business with shrewd acumen and an eye to profit. And he still saw her as his in a raw, primal way that she'd never seen in another man of her century. His to cherish. To protect. And to take, often and inventively.

He'd made another fortune trading, as she'd predicted. He'd learned English quickly and then a variety of other languages, his multilingual past making it easy for him to pick up new languages readily. Buying an identity for him and getting him legal status hadn't posed any problems. Their second and legal marriage had taken place as soon as they'd been able to arrange it. And they'd bought a house in the San Juan Islands with acreage around them, needing the quiet and the privacy. After the time spent in the past, Lorelei found the present incredibly loud and crowded and she knew it had to seem even worse to Erik. A remote and private home gave them both something like a place out of time to retreat to.

"You are mine." His fingers were thrusting in and out of her now, preparing her for another invasion. She moaned her pleasure and tried to turn towards him. He held her still. "No. I will take you like this, with your back to me."

He pulled his fingers out of her, hooked her thigh over his, and then slid his hard penis between her legs until the head pressed against her opening. She was getting more ready by the moment, but still a little tight, not fully lubricated. He knew she liked it when he took her like that, when she wasn't wet enough for him to slide inside easily and he had to work his way in with a mixture of force and persuasion.

The head pressed inside her, penetrating her. He slid one hand up to cup the underside of her breast, another hand down to stroke the now throbbing bud of her clit while he thrust into her, slowly, until he had her fully impaled.

He held still for a moment while her body adjusted to him. Then he took her ruthlessly, possessively, driving into her as hard and deep as he could. She felt the orgasm building with each thrust, getting closer, until she couldn't prevent her inner muscles from spasming and clenching around his cock as she found her release and he took his, pumping himself into her while her orgasm milked him dry.

"My woman."

The satisfaction in his voice made her smile. "Yes. Always."

Erik held his woman closer, caressing her as she recovered. "I will have to be more careful in another month or two." He cupped her belly, only slightly rounded so early in pregnancy.

She made a faint noise of exasperation. "I'm fine. You know it doesn't hurt me or the baby."

"I know that you are mine and I will take care of you." He kissed her temple, then smoothed her hair back. The length of it flowed down them both. "Sleepy?"

"Umm."

The tired response made him smile. His woman was like a cat in pregnancy, napping often, and twining around him for warmth whenever she could. "Go back to sleep, then. You have no need to rise so early this morning. I woke you only because I could wait no longer."

Her breathing shifted into the deep, even rhythm that told him she slept within minutes. Holding her while she slept, wrapped around her and buried inside her, filled him with a deep contentment he had never known until the day he'd found and taken his little slave. She completed something in him. His heart had been hers from the moment he'd set eyes on her in Hedeby, so long ago and far away. She was his heart, his life. His for all time without end.

To think that he owed it to chance. Had he not purchased the armbands from the one-eyed craftsman on one of his trading voyages, he might never have found her. The craftsman had vowed they would bring him woman-luck. Erik smiled at the woman wrapped in his protective embrace. That had been a lucky day for him, indeed.

The End

Charlene Teglia

Charlene Teglia decided she wanted to earn a living writing fiction at age twelve. After piling up enough written pages to sink Atlantis again, she sat down to write a novel and find out if it would sell. The first novel was so much fun that she got carried away and kept going, although it took another eight years to make her first novel sale. In between, she worked for various software and technology companies. She left HP when she realized she wanted to write printer repair instructions in iambic pentameter. They thought she was so funny, they left her name plate on her cube after she left like a shrine. Or maybe it was as a warning to others. She now lives with her husband and two daughters in Washington.

Learn more about Charlene's books at www.charleneteglia.com or send her an email, she'd love to hear from you! charlene@charleneteglia.com.

Samhain Publishing, Ltd.

It's all about the story...

Action/Adventure
Fantasy
Historical
Horror
Mainstream
Mystery/Suspense
Non-Fiction
Paranormal
Romance
Science Fiction
Western
Young Adult

http://www.samhainpublishing.com

Printed in the United States
57139LVS00002B/233